Going Home

Nicholasa Mohr

PUFFIN BOOKS

To Noelle Maldonado,
a third generation of Felitas
with love

I want to thank the corporation of Yaddo
for allowing me the time to work on
this book at their colony
N. M.

PUFFIN BOOKS
Published by the Penguin Group
Penguin Putnam Books for Young Readers,
345 Hudson Street, New York, New York 10014, U.S.A.
Penguin Books Ltd, 27 Wrights Lane, London W8 5TZ, England
Penguin Books Australia Ltd, Ringwood, Victoria, Australia
Penguin Books Canada Ltd, 10 Alcorn Avenue, Toronto, Ontario, Canada M4V 3B2
Penguin Books (N.Z.) Ltd, 182-190 Wairau Road, Auckland 10, New Zealand

Penguin Books Ltd, Registered Offices: Harmondsworth, Middlesex, England

First published in the United States of America by Dial Books for Young Readers,
a division of Penguin Books USA Inc., 1986
Published by Puffin Books,
a member of Penguin Putnam Books for Young Readers, 1999

17 18 19 20

THE LIBRARY OF CONGRESS HAS CATALOGED THE DIAL EDITION AS FOLLOWS:
Mohr, Nicholasa.
Going home
Summary: Feeling like an outsider when she visits her relatives in Puerto Rico
for the first time, eleven-year-old Felita finds herself having to come
to terms with the heritage she always took for granted.
[1. Puerto Ricans—New York (N.Y.)—Fiction. 2. Puerto Rico—Fiction.
3. Family life—Fiction]. I. Title.
PZ7.M72760Go 1986 [Fic] 85-20621
ISBN 0-8037-0269-8
ISBN 0-8037-0338-4 (lib. bdg.)

Puffin Books ISBN: 978-0-14-130644-5

Printed in the United States of America

Chapter

1

When my parents asked me and my brothers to come into the living room to discuss something important, I tried not to act too nervous. But, you see, ever since morning I had sensed that something strange was going on in my house by the way my parents and granduncle, Tio Jorge, kept acting. They were all whispering to each other and then when me, Johnny, or Tito came near them, they would all shut up real quick, smile, and look the other way. What was happening here anyway? I couldn't think of anything I'd done that was bad. Maybe one of my brothers had gotten into trouble. Most likely it was Tito again. I'll bet he was skipping school and got caught. Now me and Johnny would have to listen to a whole speech about it. I looked over at Tito to see if he looked guilty, but neither he or Johnny acted like they even suspected what was happening. As I sat on the couch, facing Papi, Mami, and Tio Jorge, my heart was pounding and I just hoped we weren't going to be hearing some awful news.

Papi spoke first. "Kids, we want to tell you all something—something that should make you all feel happy. You know how we've always talked about taking a trip to Puerto Rico? The whole family going there together? Well, now we are going to do it! That's right. This summer we are all gonna spend two weeks in Puerto Rico."

"That's fantastic, Papi!" said Tito. Not only was I relieved, I felt just as happy as Tito.

"When are we going?" asked Johnny.

"Right after school is over, at the beginning of July."

"I'm psyched, man!" Tito jumped up and waved his arms. "Going to P.R., far out!"

"Okay, now wait"—Papi paused—"there's something more. You know how we told you kids that Tio Jorge is retiring and has plans to live permanently in Puerto Rico? Well, the time has come; Tio will be staying in Puerto Rico and he's going to build a house in our village in the countryside. So—"

"That's right!" Tio Jorge interrupted Papi. "A

house big enough for all of you to spend time with me."

"Correct," said Papi, "and since Tio Jorge is staying, we have decided that"—Papi turned toward me —"you, Felita, will stay the whole summer in Puerto Rico and keep Tio Jorge company." When I heard those words, I could hardly believe my own ears!

"Papi, you mean I'm going away for the whole summer? Wow!" I hugged Papi, Mami, and Tio Jorge. "Thank you, everybody!"

"The most important thing," Mami said, "is that you children will finally get to meet all of your family. You have your grandfather, Abuelo Juan; your Aunt Julia and Uncle Tomás; and many cousins that you have never met. God knows"—Mami's eyes filled with tears—"I haven't seen them myself for so many years."

"Come on, Rosa"—Papi put his arm around Mami's shoulders—"this is a time for rejoicing, not for crying."

"Yeah, Mami"—Johnny reached out and squeezed Mami's hand—"we are all real happy. Right?" He looked at me and Tito.

"Sure," I agreed. I had nothing to complain about.

"Well, I'm happy too, except for one thing. How come me and Johnny only get to stay in Puerto Rico for just two weeks, and Felita gets to stay there for the whole summer? I don't think that's fair!"

"Tito, you just heard what your father said about

Tio Jorge retiring," Mami said, "and it was his wish to have Felita with him for the summer."

"Why her instead of me or Johnny? I'll tell you why, it's because she's a girl. Felita's always getting special treatment"—Tito clasped his hands over his chest and blinked, looking upward—"just because she's a girl. Big deal!"

"Cut that out!" Papi looked annoyed. "Felita is a girl, that's right! And you, you're supposed to be un macho, a young man, so stop complaining and whining like you're two years old. You sound like a sissy, you know that? You don't see your brother making any fuss. You should be happy to be going on a vacation at all!"

"Just a minute." Tio Jorge turned to Tito. "I think, and your parents agree, that it's important for Felita to spend some time in Puerto Rico. At her age it's important that she gets to learn some of the Island customs instead of just what you have here in this country and in this city. You're a young man and can take care of yourself with no problems. But with a girl it's different. Besides, you don't have to get upset, because I'm going to build my house and you can come and stay with me later on for as long as you like."

"Oh, sure, thanks a lot!" Tito snapped. "I'll probably be too old to care by then!"

"Basta!" Now Papi was real angry. "You talk to your Tio Jorge with respect, or you might find that you don't go to Puerto Rico at all. Apologize and do it right now!" Tito sat sulking. I could see he was fuming mad, but at the same time he knew that when Papi gave an order like that, he was no one to fool with.

"I'm sorry," Tito whispered.

"I'm sorry to who?" Papi asked. "And make it loud and clear!"

"I'm sorry, Tio Jorge."

"Okay. Now I don't wanna hear any more complaints coming from your mouth. Understand?" Tito nodded at Papi.

"Come on, everybody, let's stop this fighting." Mami went over to Tito and hugged him. "We are all going to enjoy ourselves so much. We are a very lucky family."

"All right, Mami." Tito smiled. Everybody knew that Tito was her favorite. If it was up to her, Tito could get away with murder and she would say he was doing a good deed.

"Listen, children," Papi said, "you are going to eat the most delicious fruits. Mangos right off the trees —so sweet and juicy. You'll see lots of flowers and green everywhere. And the weather is great. Even in the summer you always have a breeze. And of course it's never cold like here where you freeze in the winter and the humidity makes your bones ache."

They started to talk about all the fun we were gonna have. But I wasn't going to join in. Boy, was

I mad at that Tito! Right away he had to get jealous and start something about my staying in P.R. longer than him. He was always doing that. When I looked over at him, Tito gave me a dirty look. I could see he was still angry at me. Well, I wasn't gonna hang around and look at big mouth anymore. Besides, I'd already heard about how great things are in Puerto Rico. Sometimes that was all the grown-ups ever talked about. I had better things to do, like telling my friends the good news.

The first thing I did was head for the phone and call my best friend, Gigi, but there was no answer. Maybe my second best friend, Consuela, would be hanging out. Anyway, I wanted to check out my block so I could share the good news with somebody. I asked Mami if I could go out to play.

"It's cold out, Felita. What kind of games are you going to play? And besides, there's probably nobody outside now."

"Come on, Mami, you know we can play tag, hide-and-go-seek, lots of games. Or I can just hang out and talk to my friends." She always gives me a hard time about going out alone just to hang out. "Mami, please, I'd like to tell my friends about our trip. Look, if there's nobody outside, I'll come back up. I promise. Please say yes!"

"All right, but you are not to leave this block. Understand? Play on our street. No rough tomboy games. You don't hang out with boys playing boy games." Mami checked her wristwatch. "It's now two thirty. You can stay out until four, then you have to be up before it gets dark and in time for Sunday dinner. Remember, four and no later."

Actually I was relieved that Mami had given me permission to go out at all. She can be real strict sometimes and just gives me a flat no, which means I'm stuck indoors for the whole day.

There are times when I'd really like to talk to Mami and tell her how I feel, but I know she wouldn't understand my side of things. I've never been able to confide in my mother, not the way I used to with Abuelita, my grandmother. We used to talk about anything and everything. I could tell her about all the deepest secrets in my heart. Abuelita would always listen and help me solve my problems. I still missed her very much, even though it would be two years since she had died. Two years! Sometimes it felt like I'd been with her just yesterday, but at other times it seemed like she had been dead for a long time.

I put on my warm jacket, hat, and gloves so that I wouldn't freeze when I went outdoors. My street was pretty empty. Except for a passerby now and then, no one was about. Thick dark clouds covered the sky, making everything look gray and gloomy. It wasn't very windy, but it felt cold and humid. I sat down on my stoop and exhaled, watching my hot breath turn into white puffs of smoke as it hit the cold air, and I thought about Puerto Rico. All that bright sunshine every day. I shivered, feeling the cold of the stone steps going right through me, and I wondered what it must be like to live in a place where it didn't ever snow and the leaves never left the trees. I stood up, leaning against the railing, and checked my street, hoping to see somebody I could talk to about my trip.

"Hello, Felita." I turned and saw old Mrs. Sanchez coming out of our building. "It looks like snow." She smiled. "I'm off to the drugstore, the big one on the boulevard that's open on Sundays. I've got to get a prescription for Mr. Sanchez. His asthma is acting up again. You must be cold out here. I'll bet you're waiting for your friends to play with."

"Yes," I answered.

"Well, you children have a good time. Bye."

"Bye," I said, wishing someone I could talk to would hurry up and come by. And then I saw Consuela and her little sister, Joanie, coming up the block. I waved at them, calling them over. "Have I got great news to tell you!"

"What's up?" asked Joanie. She has to be the nosiest little girl in the whole world. I was really speaking to Consuela, her older sister. One of these days I hoped Consuela wouldn't have to mind Joanie so we could have our conversations in private.

"Remember I told you my Tio Jorge was gonna retire and live in Puerto Rico? And that we all might get to go too? Well, it's true! But wait, here's the best part. Johnny and Tito are coming back with my parents after two weeks there, but I'll be spending the whole summer in P.R. I'm going to live with my tio in his village."

"Wow," Consuela said. I could see Consuela and Joanie were impressed. That made me very happy.

"When are you going?" asked Joanie.

"Oh, not till the end of school. Around the beginning of July."

"Man, that's a long long way off," Joanie said, sounding disappointed. "I thought you was going right away."

"Don't be so stupid." That Joanie could get on your nerves. "I have to wait until school finishes." I turned to Consuela, ignoring Joanie. "I wanted to let my good friends know."

"Does Gigi know yet?" asked Consuela.

"I tried to telephone her, but no one was home. I'll try again later. If she's not in, I'll tell her tomorrow in person."

"Hey, Felita!" I turned and saw the twins, Dan and Duane Gonzalez. They are in my same grade in school. They look so much alike that the only way you can tell them apart is that Duane has darker skin than Dan. I waved for them to come over, and told them about my trip.

"Boy, are you lucky, girl," said Dan. "I'd sure like to go."

"Me too," Duane said. "Our parents are always talking about Puerto Rico. We got a mess of relatives down there, according to them. But neither me or Dan have ever been there."

"I was born there, you know," Consuela said proudly, "but I came here when I was real little."

"Do you remember anything from there?" asked Dan.

"No, I was just a baby when we moved here. I don't remember nothing. But I heard a lot of stories about life there."

We were all having a real good time talking about P.R., when all of a sudden I see my brother Tito coming out of our building. Without even a greeting to anybody, he blurts out, "Get upstairs, Felita. Mami wants you now!"

"How come now? She said I could stay out till four and I know it can't be four o'clock yet."

"It's three thirty, but so what?" he said. "Mami sent me to get a few things for her at the bodega and she told me to tell you to get home. Right now."

"I bet she did not," I responded. "I bet she only told you to remind me to get upstairs on time."

"Listen." Tito stood very close to me. "You better do like I say. Soon it'll be time to eat. Put on some speed, girl. You know I'm supposed to look after you, so that makes me in charge. Now get your butt upstairs!" Butt? I couldn't believe it! Who did that Tito think he was anyway?

"I will not!" I stared right back at him. "I got till four and I'll go up then. You get Mami to tell me to go up, dumbo!"

Tito put his face real close to mine, then he clenched his fists and began to shout at me, "You want me to make you?" He had a way of sticking his chin way out and looking real mean and ugly. I knew that he might just take a swipe at me so he could look tough in front of everybody. Tito was so gross! I shook my head, looking real disgusted at him, and decided I better leave before things got nasty.

"I gotta go up anyway," I told everyone. "But not because dumbo here says so. It's almost time to eat, and I gotta do a few personal things." I walked away real slow, trying not to act like I was following Tito's orders. But I was really so embarrassed. Lately he's been doing too much of that. He's only thirteen . . . two measly years older than me. Yet he's always bossing me every chance he gets. I was really beginning to hate him.

When I got upstairs, I went straight to Mami and asked her if she had really sent Tito to get me. Right away she goes into one of her speeches defending Tito and making everything my fault.

"Mira, Felita, you are no longer a baby, you are a young lady who is not supposed to be out playing like a tomboy. There are all kinds of títeres out there in the street—no-good hoodlums that can harm you. Your brothers are looking out for your own protection. They have to be responsible and check on you when you are out of the house."

"But you said I could stay out till four. So who's Tito to tell me to come up at three thirty? What makes him so—"

"Stop it, Felita! Your brothers are older and they are boys. Honestly, I don't understand you kids here today. I mean, back home in Puerto Rico boys respect girls, and girls know their place. What would people say if I let you run loose like one of those girls no one respects, eh? You know that you are allowed to play with girls, or in a mixed group of boys and girls. And consider yourself very, very lucky that I let you go out by yourself at all!"

I wanted to ask her what that had to do with Tito coming and bossing me around in front of my friends. But I knew that all Mami would do was repeat this same speech, always finding new ways of saying the some old things, and it was always for "my own good." But she couldn't convince me that having two bullies for brothers was going to make it any safer or better for me.

Actually ever since my eleventh birthday last November, things had been getting worse between us. That's when Mami told me that I would soon be getting my period and I would become a woman. Actually I already knew all about it. Mrs. Rose in Hygiene had explained to the whole class about the menstrual cycle. It was a good thing too, because what Mami had told me would have made me think that if a boy ever touched me in my private parts, I could get pregnant. She had sat me down, saying I had to hear about the facts of life so I could protect myself. She told me I must be very careful, and had to guard myself from then on. I could not act like before, and grab my brothers and jump all over them, or sit on everybody's lap like I was still a little girl. That all had to stop. That's why my brothers would have to watch out for me and make sure I was safe.

From that time on Mami started keeping strict tabs on me. I couldn't play outdoors as much as I used to, and she also wanted to know where I was practically every single minute. If I wasn't where I was supposed to be all the time, it became my fault. It seemed like everything I did was wrong and that I was always to blame. Now sometimes even when I play in a mixed group of boys and girls, I feel I'm doing something bad. What was the use? When it came to my feelings and my personal thoughts, Mami was definitely no person to talk to.

Without another word I walked away and went to my own room. It's so small you can hardly turn around in it. But one nice thing is that out of my window I can see part of the park and a nice chunk of sky. It was beginning to snow. The flakes were very tiny and wet, and they melted as soon as they touched the ground. I stood close to the window, leaning as far to the left as possible so I could see past the park entrance over to the playground and the baseball field where some of us kids play when there are no other games going on. It was empty and deserted now. I looked down at the street, three stories below. There was hardly anybody out except for some people who hurried along, trying to avoid the cold. I thought about telling Papi what Tito had just done to me, bossing me around in front of my friends. Maybe after dinner I'd talk to him. Even though most of the time my father isn't much more help than Mami, at least he hears me out.

"Felita, Felita! It's dinnertime." I heard Mami calling me and went out into the kitchen. Johnny, Tito, and Tio Jorge were already seated, but not Papi.

"Where's Papi?" I asked.

"He's working today at the plant," said Mami. "They asked him to fill in on the evening shift for somebody who couldn't make it today."

"I hate it when he works so much overtime and can't be with us," I said.

"None of us like it either, Felita, but we can use the extra money now that we're going to Puerto Rico. We're all going to have to save and understand that this vacation is going to be a big expense for the family." Mami finished serving the food and sat down.

"Ma," Tito said, "can I take my food into the living room? There's a sports special on that I really have to see."

"Tito, you know your father doesn't like that. He wants us all to eat together at the dinner table."

"Yeah, but he ain't here now. So please can I watch T.V.?"

"Tito, I don't like it myself. I prefer that you eat with us."

"Oh, man." Tito pushed his plate away. "I'm not hungry. Can I be excused? I'd rather go to my room."

"Tito, no te pongas tonto. Stop being silly and eat your food."

"Mami, come on. What's the difference if I'm here? This is a very important program. They got my favorite teams playing. Look, I promise that I'll wash my plate so clean that when you pick it up, you'll say, 'Oh, my! Look, I can see my own beautiful reflection'—just like on the T.V. commercials. I swear!" Mami began to laugh. "Please, Ma," Tito persisted. "Pretty please."

"All right." Mami gave in. "Go on. But don't be making a habit of it. You know Sunday dinner is for all of us to eat together." Tito jumped up, kissed Mami, then grabbed his plate and rushed out.

"He always gets his way. Why do you let him do what he wants?" I was really angry. "If I ask for something, you never—"

"Don't start." Mami cut me off. "Just eat your food."

"If Papi were here, Tito wouldn't get away with eating and watching T.V. I'll bet that Papi would—"

"Basta! Enough!" Mami looked annoyed. "Do me a favor, Felita, change the subject. Not another word about it. Do you hear?" I looked at my oldest brother, who shrugged and smiled sympathetically. Even though Johnny can be a pest at times . . . I still like him. He's not mean to me like Tito. In fact since he's sixteen and bigger than Tito, he comes to my defense when he sees Tito bullying me. But that Tito is sneaky and he usually waits till there's no one around to pick on me.

Everyone at the table was eating in silence. Finally Mami spoke to Johnny. "How's the science report coming along?"

"All right. I have to do more work at the library, reading and researching, but I'll get it in on time." Johnny is a very good student, which makes my parents very happy. Tito, on the other hand, is a very poor student, which worries my parents all the time.

"Tio Jorge, have some more chicken," Mami was saying. "There's plenty left."

"No, thank you, Rosa." Tio isn't much for talking. He's very shy. Papi said Tio Jorge has always been that way. Sometimes I wonder if he even hears what goes on. Tio Jorge's theory is that he doesn't believe in hablando de tonterias—talking about nonsense— which to him means talking about anything except his nature collection. He's real proud of that collection. It took him years to assemble, probably all his life. He has tons of pictures, cards, slides, and books all about trees, flowers, birds, and butterflies. Sometimes I think that that's all he ever cares about.

Papi says that ever since Abuelita died, Tio has become even more shy. Like he's always in his own private little world. Abuelita was Tio's older sister and he lived with her for all of his life, until she passed away, of course. Then he moved in with us. At the beginning he used to complain about a lot of things to Mami and talk about how Abuelita used to do his white shirts herself instead of sending them out to a laundry. Or how Abuelita used real cream instead of milk when she cooked the hot cereals.

Mami used to get so upset until Papi told her that Tio was just old and set in his ways and she should ignore him and go about her business as usual. In time Tio stopped complaining.

No one at the dinner table was in a talkative mood. Mami kept trying to start a conversation, but all she got from us was a no or a yes. I finished eating and asked to be excused.

"Do you want more dessert, Felita? There's more bread pudding left. I know how much you like it." Now she was being nice to me, but if I complained to her about Tito, she'd come right to his defense.

"No," I answered.

"Are you sure?" Mami reached out to refill my plate.

"May I please be excused?" I stood up.

"Felita, if there is something the matter, tell me what it is."

"Nothing is the matter. I just want to leave and go to my room!"

Mami looked at me and shook her head. "Go on, then."

I took my dishes to the sink and left. Weekdays I'm the one who helps Mami with the dishes. Saturday and Sunday, Johnny and Tito take turns helping her. I was glad today was Sunday because it meant I didn't have to stay and be forced to talk to her.

Back in my room I thought of Papi and wished he didn't have to work so much overtime. It's always better when he's at home. Somehow with him here the family feels more complete. Plus then Tito can't get away with as much. But lately I was getting pretty fed up with Papi too. Like just last week when I complained to him about my brothers, he began to sound just like Mami. He told me I would soon be a señorita, and said that Johnny and Tito want to make sure that no boys will take advantage of me.

When I told Papi that nobody I knew of was taking advantage of me except for my brothers themselves, and especially Tito, it didn't seem to change his mind one bit. "Girls do not have the same freedom as boys," Papi said. "That's the law of nature."

"What law of nature is that?" I protested. "I'm every bit as good as them, even better. And I can take care of myself. I don't need them for nothing!"

At this Papi got real angry and cut short the conversation. "Basta! I don't want to hear that kind of talk. It's a fact that you cannot take care of yourself, even if you think you can. Understand? Now, that's all there is to it."

I had felt so angry and humiliated that when Papi reached out to make up, I had stepped away from him and left the room. Remembering all of this, I realized I just had to learn to handle things by myself.

My one and only ally, when he came out of his own world, was Tio Jorge. Last Thursday, for example, when I was watching T.V., Tito walked into the living room and switched the channel without even saying one word. When I tried to turn the dial back to my program, Tito started a fight. Right away he shoved me, but I shoved him right back. Luckily Tio was there and came to my rescue. "Get out!" he told Tito. "I don't want you in this room. Don't you dare touch your sister."

Tito had looked mean, like he was going to give Tio Jorge a hard time, but he thought better of it. He knew that if he misbehaved with Tio Jorge he'd have to account to Papi. I was real pleased when he shut his mouth and left the room. But usually that's not what happens. Usually Tito gets his way.

I looked over at my clock radio, a present my parents had given me last Christmas. It was already six o'clock. I was feeling bored, and even though I had decided to wait till tomorrow to tell Gigi about my trip, I was really tempted to telephone her right away. But then I heard a knock on my door. "Come in," I said.

The door opened slightly. "It's me, Tio. May I come in?"

"Sure." I was surprised. Tio Jorge hardly ever came into my room. He shut the door and sat next to me.

"Felita, are you happy to be going to Puerto Rico?"

"Oh, yes, very happy, Tio."

"Good. I'm glad because I want to be able to teach you about nature. I can't teach you about those things here. You will learn about all kinds of trees, flowers, and birds. You'll also see life in a different way in our village."

I knew Tio had come in to cheer me up. But he seemed sad, even unhappy. "Tio, aren't you happy to be going?"

"Sí, of course I am happy." He smiled. "I'm going home, Felita, that's where I want to be—home in the countryside where I belong, in my village of Barrio Antulio, where I will be close to nature. That's where I was born and grew up, where I'll spend the rest of my days, meet my maker. I'm not at home here in this country, and I never was. Now, Abuelita, your grandmother, that one liked it here. She enjoyed the city. That's how come we stayed as long as we did.

Now I'm going back. . . ." But he still sounded sad to me.

"Well, Tio, I can't wait to go and I'm real happy that I can stay with you for the whole summer." I put my arms around him and gave him a hug.

"Good." He got up slowly and left.

I looked out the window and saw that the snow was coming down heavily. Sometimes the flakes fell in bunches, separating in midair like white powder. The lampposts, stoops, cars, and sidewalks, just about everything, were covered with snow. Long dark silver shadows stretched out over the whiteness. Usually I prayed for a storm so that school would be shut down and we could all play outdoors—have snowball fights, build tunnels, and just hang out, not having to worry about classes or taking tests. But this evening I wanted the snow to stop so that to-morrow I could tell all my friends about my trip to Puerto Rico.

2

The next day I met Consuela and Joanie down near the corner of the large intersection. As usual we all walked to school together. It was routine that we met every morning, because too many tough kids can pick on you if you walk by yourself. There was safety in numbers. I was so happy to see my wish had come true: the sun was shining and melting the snow away. Some kids were busy hollering, sliding, and jumping all over the place, trying to have snowball fights. But the snow was so powdery that most of the balls fell apart even before they got thrown.

This morning I had gotten permission to go over

to Gigi's house after school. Gigi's mother is the most easygoing mother I know. I am welcome to visit them anytime, just as long as I get Mami's okay. Gigi's mother even takes me shopping with them and buys me treats and lunch. I call her by her first name and so does Gigi. Before I used to call her Mrs. Mercado, but last year she insisted I call her Doris. When I had told Mami that, she said she thought it was disrespectful, and that Mrs. Mercado must think she was Gigi's sister instead of her mother. But I don't care how Mami feels. I love being with Doris and Gigi because I can be myself. I can say whatever pops into my head and not have to worry about getting an argument back.

When we got to class, I sat next to Gigi and whispered the good news about my trip. Then I added, "Can I come over to your house after school? I got permission."

"Great." She nodded.

I could hardly keep my mind on my schoolwork, and when lunchtime came around, I was practically jumping out of my skin. We have our tight little group in school. There is Gigi, Consuela, Elba Thomas, Lydia Cortez, and Vivian Montañez. Today we all sat together like always. I waited for just the right moment, after everyone was settled and munching away.

"Guess what, everybody? I'm going to Puerto Rico for the whole summer!" I announced.

"Wow!" said Elba.

"Really? That's great!" Vivian said. Right away everybody became interested.

"When are you going exactly?" asked Lydia.

"Not until school is over. We're all leaving early in July. My parents and brothers are only staying two weeks, but I'm going to—"

"Oh, man, look! There he is. There's Vinny!" Vivian interrupted me, and everyone turned away to look at Vinny Davila as he walked by and waved at us.

"He's so cute," Vivian went on. "I just love his eyes." She kept on waving at him longer than anybody else with a smile stuck on her face and her teeth hanging out. I tried to get back their attention so I could talk about my trip, but now there was no way they would listen. Everyone was more interested in Vinny, the new boy from Colombia, South America. He had registered at our school only at the beginning of last month. His real name was Vicente Davila, but he had asked everyone to call him Vinny, which he pronounced "Veenie." Naturally we all knew he meant Vinny, but that Joey Ramos and his dumb gang of friends took advantage of him and made fun of him. They imitated his accent and called him "Beenie." That really made me mad.

Vinny's English was so bad that they put him back. That's why even though he's a year older than our group, he's in our grade. I heard he's the oldest of five kids. He lives right on my block so I usually see him walking to and from school, but so far I've never seen him hanging out. He has jet black hair and fair skin with freckles. All the girls think he's real cute. And even though I never said it, I gotta admit he's a very handsome boy. But I'm glad he's not in my class. You see, I really can't stand it when all my girlfriends act so silly over boys.

Like right now, for instance, here I am trying to say something important about my trip, and they all don't even care.

"Like I was saying," I went on. "My brothers are leaving early, which makes me happy. My Tio Jorge says we'll be going for hikes and to the beach and—"

"Oh, look, here he comes again. Look!" Vivian cut me off a second time and began to giggle. "He's coming our way. Oh, I can't stand it!" She kept right on grinning at him.

"I think you're the one he's looking at, Vivian," said Elba.

"I sure hope so." Vivian sighed. "Like who cares if his English stinks. I could teach him how to talk better real quick." All the girls began to laugh and were now grinning at Vinny like fools. All except Gigi. She just looked at me and rolled back her eyes. By now I was pretty furious. It was like what I had to say was not the least bit important because Vinny came around. All right, I thought, just wait until they all have something important they want me to hear. I'll show them.

"I guess you all are not interested in my trip or care about what I was saying." I looked directly at Vivian.

"Felita, you ain't even going until the summer," she said, "and we all got plenty of time to hear about your trip."

I was so annoyed at her. "Hey, I'm not twisting any arms, so you all don't have to listen. I only figured as my very best friends you'd like to hear about my good news. That's all!"

"We are interested, Felita," said Elba, "go on and tell us." I remained silent until they all had to ask me again.

"We're all ears," said Lydia.

"All right, then." I was too happy thinking about my trip to stay angry. But there wasn't much time left before lunch was over and we had to get back to class.

After school Gigi and I went over to her house. Last year her parents had bought a big apartment in a development that was a twenty-minute walk from school. It was drizzling out and the leftover snow was turning into rivers of brown mush and disappearing into the drain holes and sewers. The dampness and cold made us shiver. Gigi and I linked our arms and huddled together to keep warm. We walked so fast that we were practically running.

"Imagine, living in a place where it never gets cold," I said.

"I can't imagine," Gigi said. "Not on a day like today."

When we got to Gi's house, Doris gave us hot chocolate and cookies. The three of us sat in the kitchen, where it was warm and cozy.

"Bueno," Doris said, "what a lucky girl you are to be going on such a long vacation to Puerto Rico."

"I know." I sure was feeling pleased. "I already heard so many stories about P.R., ever since I was little. My abuelita told me that everything is so beautiful—the flowers, mountains . . ."

"It's beautiful all right, but it's also changed a lot since your grandmother's time," said Doris. "I know because when I went there for a visit eight years ago, I found things were a whole lot different than when I was young."

"Oh, but you see, my Tio Jorge says that we'll be living in his village and that not much has changed there."

"What's the difference? I know you'll have a great time anyway, Felita."

"I wish I could go with Felita," said Gigi.

"Someday we're all going, but we just bought this apartment and you know your father and I can't afford any trips now. But we will have a family reunion in Puerto Rico one day, and you'll meet all your relatives there, Gigi. I promise."

"Great, Doris." Gigi kissed her mother. "When is Daddy coming home?"

"Thursday of next week. He wrote that he's bringing us something special." Gigi's father is a merchant seaman who is away for many weeks at a time. But when he comes home from a trip, it's so much fun, almost like having a celebration. He brings all kinds of pretty things for their home and gifts for Gigi and Doris. Sometimes he gives me something too. Last time I got a bottle of toilet water that smelled like roses.

After we finished eating, Gigi and I went to her room. She has such a big room. It's at least three times the size of my cubbyhole. They even have two bathrooms in their apartment. Would I love to have two bathrooms in my house! Everybody is always fighting to get to the toilet first, or waiting to get in. I can never sit down in peace without somebody banging on the door. In her room Gigi has her own portable color T.V., and last month her father got her a new cassette player.

"You are so lucky, Gigi. I wish I had some of the things you have. Especially my own T.V. Do you know what a pain it is to watch programs everybody else likes except you? When my brothers take over with their sports programs, it's like nothing else matters."

"But it must be so nice to have two older brothers. It gets lonely being an only child, you know. Nobody to talk to or play with."

"Are you kidding? Who talks to my brothers? Or plays with them? All they do is boss me around and tell me what to do. Mostly we fight." I looked around her room. "I wish I was an only child so I could have all these great things for my very own private use."

"I don't know, but sometimes I would trade in all of this for a brother or sister. When I was little, I always used to ask my parents for a baby sister or brother. First they used to tell me that in the future God would bring me one, but as I got older and kept on asking, they finally told me the truth. There was not gonna be any more kids in this family, they told me. Like I was it. They said that this way they could afford to give me the best of everything, and that they just couldn't afford no more kids."

"That sounds like a good idea to me. I could do without Tito, even Johnny sometimes, and in that order."

"Well"—Gigi shook her head—"I still wish I had a sister."

"But you and I are sisters. Don't you remember the pact we made in first grade? We agreed then that we would always be sisters, and so we are."

"True." Gigi looked real sad. "I'm gonna miss you so much, Felita. I wish I could go with you." Now we both became quiet and sad, thinking about being separated.

"Wait a minute. I'm only going for the summer

and I'm not even leaving till July, and it's only March. So why are we feeling so sad?"

"Right!" Gigi laughed, and we hugged.

Gigi walked me part of the way home. I had to get back before five. It still got dark out early and Mami always worried and became nervous if I wasn't home on time. But I also don't like walking home by myself, especially when it's dark out. Sometimes a smelly bum all dirty and drunk comes over to ask for money or some tough kids try to start an argument.

Gigi and I said good-bye by the large boulevard, and I rushed across the street, putting on some speed.

"Felita! Mira, Felita, espera . . . espera un momento!" I heard my name and someone calling out to me in Spanish to wait up. Turning around, I saw Vinny Davila. He was waving as he hurried over. "Hello, are you going home?" he asked me in Spanish. I nodded. "Can I walk along with you, please?"

"Sure." I shrugged. I wasn't expecting to see Vinny. It felt strange walking with Vinny because I hardly knew him or had ever really had a conversation with him. The rain had stopped and the sharp wind sent a chill right through my coat. Neither of us said anything. I kept waiting for him to say something, but he just walked silently alongside me. Finally I decided to break the ice by speaking first, in Spanish. "How do you like it in this country so far?"

"I like it." He smiled. "I'm learning and seeing new things every day." We continued to speak in Spanish.

"That's very good. Do you like school here?"

"Yes, except for my English, which is pretty lousy. I wanna work on it so that I can speak it fluently just like all the other kids."

"It must be hard to come here from another country and have to learn to speak a different language right away. You know, my grandmother lived here for something like forty years and she never learned to speak English fluently."

"Well, I sure hope I do better than your grandmother!" We both burst out laughing. "How does she manage to get along without speaking English?"

"Oh, she passed away. She's been dead for two years. She was very intelligent and could solve people's problems. My grandmother was the most wonderful person I ever met. We spoke in Spanish all the time, just like you and me are doing right now. Abuelita used to even read to me in Spanish."

"You speak Spanish very well, Felita."

"Not as well as I used to. I know I make mistakes, but I like speaking it."

"You are Puerto Rican, right?"

"Right, born here. My parents are from the Island. I guess you can tell from my accent in Spanish." My accent in Spanish was different from his. Vinny spoke slowly and pronounced his words carefully, while us Puerto Ricans speak much faster.

"I noticed that most of the kids in school are Puerto Rican too, yet many don't speak Spanish as well as you do. Did you ever live in Puerto Rico, Felita?"

"No, I've never been there. But it's funny that you asked me that because guess what? I'm going to be spending the whole summer there. It will be my first visit. I can't wait!"

"That's wonderful! I wish I could speak English the way you speak Spanish, Felita. You know I really want to learn. And, frankly, that's why I came looking for you, to see if you could help me out. Can you help me, Felita? To speak English I mean?"

"What?" I couldn't believe he was asking me to help him.

"Look," he went on, "I'll be honest with you. I've been watching you and I see the way you work. You are a good student. You're always in the library, studying. And the way you draw is terrific. Those pictures that you have on display are great. See, I've been trying to talk to somebody, like one of the other students, but I just didn't know who to ask. Then I noticed you and watched you and thought, all right, she's the one! Felita is really smart and speaks Spanish, so I can talk to her."

Vinny stopped and looked at me with a hurt expression. "Some of the other students make fun of me and call me names. I want to speak correctly. I don't want to stay speaking English the way I do now. Will you help me, Felita?"

"Me—but how?" I couldn't imagine what I could do to help.

"Teach me to speak English just like you and the other kids do."

"You know, Vinny, they got extra classes in school where foreign people learn English. I know because some of my parents' friends from Puerto Rico went there. Let me ask for you. Maybe they might even give you special instructions because you are a kid. Tomorrow I'll ask Mr. Richards—"

"No"—he cut me off—"I'm not interested in learning any more grammar or English out of books. I can do that myself. What I need is to talk like any other kid. Not out of books, but just regular conversation. Will you help me, please?"

"I still don't know what I can do." I was getting pretty confused.

"It's very simple. We can meet after school, not each day, but perhaps two times a week. We can just talk about anything. This way I can begin to sound like everybody else."

"I really don't know about that." Vinny stopped and stood before me, his pale green eyes staring sadly at me.

"Please. Look, Felita, you say that you are going to Puerto Rico this summer. And that your Spanish isn't all that good, right? Well, what if I help you out with Spanish? Wouldn't you like to speak it better and learn to read and write it? In this way we can help each other out."

I thought about his offer and felt a rush of excitement going right through me. Imagine, out of all the kids in our school, it was going to be me teaching English to Vinny Davila, who all my girlfriends like and act silly around and drool over. The more I thought about it, the more it seemed almost too good to be true. And then I remembered my parents, especially Mami. How could I ever convince her I should have lessons with a boy? And worse yet, a stranger she'd never even met!

"Don't you think it's a good idea, Felita?"

"Sure I do. In fact I miss not being able to speak to my grandmother in Spanish, and I am going to Puerto Rico, so I would like to speak it as good as possible."

"So, do we have a deal?" I didn't know how to answer Vinny. I mean tackling Mami was a heavy order, and yet I didn't want to say no to this opportunity of having lessons with Vinny Davila.

"Let me talk to my mother and see what I can do." I could hardly believe what I'd just heard myself say.

"Wonderful! Thank you so much!" Vinny got so excited he spun around and clapped a few times.

"Hey, wait a minute, Vinny. I'm telling you right

now I can't make any promises. I still have to figure out a few things and get permission."

"All right, but you will let me know soon?"

"I'll let you know when I know what's happening. We can talk in school in a free period or you can come to the library when I'm there, okay?"

"That's really great. Thank you so much." He paused and glanced at me, looking a little embarrassed. "There's just one more thing. I don't want the other kids in school to know about our lessons—at least not in the beginning. I'd like to wait until I'm speaking better in English. Can we keep this to ourselves?"

"Sure," I said. This was even better than I thought. The fact that Vinny Davila and me shared a secret made me feel special.

"I have to run or I'll be late." I turned and ran up the steps. "See you!" I called out to him in English.

"See you!" I heard his voice echoing me in English.

Boy, what just happened, anyway? Here I had just agreed to have lessons with Vinny Davila. I couldn't believe it and inside my stomach it felt like butterflies were doing flip-flops. I couldn't get over the fact that he needed my help. At home I looked at myself in the mirror. I know he thinks I'm smart, but maybe he thinks I'm pretty too. I wished my eyes were bigger like Vivian's and that my nose was nice and straight like Consuela's instead of looking like a button on my face. Oh, well, I was glad Vinny liked my drawings. I had done two big drawings to celebrate Lincoln's and Washington's birthdays. I had copied the scenes from a magazine, but naturally I had added my own special touches so that they wouldn't be plain old copies. When I thought of the girls at school, especially Vivian, I got a case of the giggles. Wait till she hears that Vinny Davila, who she moans and groans over, has asked me to help him! Too much!

The more I thought about this whole business, the more anxious I got wondering how to work it out with Mami. I had to think very carefully now and plan things so that they would turn out just right. I had one lucky break—Papi was home. With him here I could at least argue my case. Getting my parents to listen without my brothers hearing us was next to impossible. In our small apartment there was always somebody in the living room or kitchen and everyone could hear what you said. I decided to bring it out in the open, and the best time would be tonight when everybody would be in a good mood because Papi was home.

At supper Mami and Papi were talking about the trip. I listened, waiting for the right moment.

"I already wrote to my sister Julia," Mami said, "and to my father. God, to think we have three children growing up without knowing their own family. Julia's boys are almost Tito and Johnny's ages, and my brother Tomás's boy and girl are a little younger than Felita. Imagine how happy my father is going to be. He keeps on saying in his letters that all he wants before he dies is to see his grandchildren."

"Rosa, that man is as healthy as an ox," said Papi. "Not many men outlive two wives and then get married for a third time at age seventy. He'll live a long time yet."

"I know. My father is something else all right! But it's going to be so good for all of us. This family reunion has been long overdue."

"I can't wait to meet my cousins," I said, thinking it was a good time to start, "but I wonder if they know how to speak English?"

"Felita"—Mami looked surprised—"you know that in Puerto Rico people speak Spanish. That's the language there."

"Well, Felita has a point," said Papi, "because they teach English in school. And anyway, what with all the traveling back and forth from the Island to here, I'm sure by now most people know some English."

"I sure hope so." I sighed.

"Felita, but you understand Spanish," said Tio Jorge, "and you also speak it pretty good. All them years talking to your grandmother must have taught you something."

"Yeah, but Abuelita's been dead for two years and I don't hardly speak it anymore."

"Your brothers are in the same situation, and they don't look worried to me. Do you, boys?" Papi looked at Johnny and Tito.

"I haven't even thought about it, Papi," said

Johnny. "Besides, I understand almost everything, and I'm taking it in school. Remember?"

"I'm doing real good in Spanish. It's one of my best subjects," Tito said. "I'll make myself understood in P.R. No sweat."

"Felita, are you really worried?" Tio asked. I nodded. "Well, then we can speak in Spanish from now on. That should help you."

It's now or never, I thought. Go for it! "Something even better came up." Everybody stopped eating and looked at me. "You see, there's this new kid in our school. He just registered last month. He comes from Colombia in South America, you know." I told them about Vinny and his problem with learning English and how the kids make fun of him. "He got this idea that I could help him with his English and in exchange he could help me with my Spanish. Sort of a trade-off, you know." I paused and waited, but no one said anything. "I really think it's a great idea, especially since I'm going to Puerto Rico and it will help me when I have to talk Spanish there." My mother was speechless, then she looked at my father, who smiled and shrugged.

"Is that the boy that lives right here on our block?" Johnny asked me.

"Yeah, that's him. His name is Vinny Davila. He lives down the block, near the other corner from us, but across the street."

"Do you know him?" Papi asked Johnny.

"I've just seen him around, that's all. But he seems like a good kid. He always says hello when he sees me."

"I seen him too," said Tito. "You remember, Ma. We both seen the whole family. That time when we came from shopping last week, and you said they seem like nice people?"

"Oh, that's right." My mother nodded. "I remember now. But why can't this boy get extra help in English from the schools where there are teachers trained for that? Why do you have to give him lessons, Felita? Since when have you become an English teacher!"

"Because, Mami, he wants to learn conversation—how to talk regular English like the rest of us kids. He doesn't want an English teacher. That's the whole point! Teachers ain't going to be able to teach him like another kid can. Right, Johnny?"

"Maybe so." Johnny looked like he almost agreed.

"Well, I think Felita is right. There are certain things you ain't gonna get in school." When I heard Tito say this, I was almost shocked out of my chair. My jaw just about dropped to the floor. Man, I don't remember the last time Tito had been on my side for anything!

"Sure you would say that"—Papi shook his head —"our number-one student here! Since when, Tito, are you an expert on school?"

"Aw, man, Papi," Tito spoke up, "come on, admit she's got a point. The kid wants to be accepted, to be like one of us. That's all. All the other kids will keep right on teasing him until he learns our ways. That's just the way it is, and he ain't gonna learn regular expressions and how to fit in with other kids from a teacher."

"Papi, Tito is right," I said. "And it wouldn't be no trouble, honest. We could meet like twice a week after school and spend an hour or so working on conversations. Me teaching him English and him teaching me Spanish."

"But why can't he learn from another boy?" I knew Mami would ask something like that. "There are plenty of boys in that school, chica. Why you?"

"Mami, first of all most of the boys make mean fun of him, real nasty fun, and second he asked me because I do speak Spanish. This way we can communicate. Plus here's the best part. He can really help me with my Spanish, which is pretty rusty by now. He even said he'll teach me to read and write in Spanish. It would really help me when I get to P.R. Remember, I'm going to have to be there for the whole summer with people who probably don't speak English." I waited and no one said anything. I stared at Papi, silently pleading my case.

"It can't do no harm, Rosa," said Papi.

"Where are these lessons going to take place, then, young lady?" asked Mami.

"We can meet here if you like, or in his house. Anywhere you say, Mami."

"I don't know, let me think about it." I knew I couldn't let her think about it even for one second. She had to agree before we all left the table.

"Aw, come on, Mami, it'll all be for a good cause. He can learn English and I can learn Spanish." I turned to my father. "Please, Papi! Come on, what's wrong with such a great idea?" Papi smiled, and I knew right then I had to get his okay.

"Look," I said, "we can try it and if you see anything wrong, anything at all, or if you don't like Vinny, we'll stop. Honest, I swear. What's bad about that?"

"It's okay with me if it's all right with your mother."

I turned toward my mother. "Mami? Say it's okay. Please, please!"

"Bueno . . . okay." My mother heaved a big sigh. "But we just try it, that's all, and then see how it goes. There is nothing definite, you understand?"

"Terrific. Thanks, Mami! Vinny will really be happy."

"And if you want to practice Spanish with me, you just let me know," said Tio Jorge.

"Thank you, I will, Tio."

"We'll look out for her, Mami," said Johnny. That really annoyed me. Nobody had asked for his two cents. But I thought I'd better leave things alone, since everything was going good. Tito, to my surprise, said nothing. I looked up at him, and when our eyes met, I silently thanked him.

Mami decided that Vinny and I would meet after school at four o'clock on Mondays and Thursdays and work for an hour. The lessons would be at my house. After a few weeks, if everything worked out okay between Vinny and me, we could talk about alternating one week at my house and one week at his house. But for now lessons were to be right in our living room, where Mami could watch us.

It was Thursday of the first week and we were up to our second lesson. As I was waiting for Vinny, I overheard Mami talking to Tio Jorge. "That boy has wonderful manners, Tio Jorge, and it's a pleasure talking with him. There is something about the way children are brought up in a Latino culture that is missing here. They are taught to respect their elders. Imagine, Vinny is only twelve and already he's un hombrecito. I wish our Tito acted as well. That's why I'm glad we are all going to Puerto Rico and that Felita will be staying the whole summer. Maybe my kids will learn and see things the way we used to."

"He's a good boy, Rosa," Tio Jorge agreed. "I'm going to invite him to look at my nature collection." When I heard that, I knew Tio Jorge liked Vinny, because he doesn't offer to show his collection to just anybody.

I had to admit that I was really beginning to like Vinny. And I mean a lot; like maybe more than friends. But I didn't want to become all gushy and dopey like the way my girlfriends acted with him at school. And besides, I didn't even know if he liked me—in that way, I mean. The whole idea made me so nervous that I decided I wasn't gonna think about it too much. I'd just concentrate real hard on our lessons and see what happened.

When Vinny came, he brought me two books in Spanish—a second grade reader and a book of children's stories with colorful pictures. I found that I could read and understand most of the children's stories, but with the reader there were a lot of words and phrases I didn't quite get. This weekend my brother Johnny was taking me to a bookstore where we could buy a Spanish/English dictionary. Tio Jorge had given me the money for it. He figured I should be well prepared in Spanish when I got to Puerto Rico.

When Vinny lived in Colombia, he had seen the Star Wars movies and really loved them. After I told him I had all the paperbacks—*Star Wars, The Empire Strikes Back*, and *Return of the Jedi*—he got real excited and asked if we could work with these books. I had dug them out and now I gave them to him. But he just nodded and looked upset.

"Hey, what's up? I thought you wanted these

books," I said. Most of the time we still spoke in Spanish.

"I do, it's not that. In fact they're really great. It's something else." He sounded real serious.

"What else?"

"Felita, you gotta help me with a word that's not in the English dictionary."

"Sure. What is it?"

"It's called 'bimbo.' "

"Where did you hear that?" I started laughing, but he got so upset that I stopped.

"Joey Ramos and some of the other boys stopped me and told me I was going to have a new nickname. From now on, they said, they were calling me 'Bimbo Vinny.' They said it means being smart. But I figured they were lying and it probably means something else, something bad. Am I right?"

"You're right, Vinny, it doesn't mean smart. It means just the opposite—stupid or dummy."

"You see? I was right! I knew it just by the expressions on their faces and the way they were all laughing."

"What did you do?"

"Don't worry, I stood up to them and spoke to them in English. I said, 'No way! You don't call me this. Please to call me by my name. Vinny, understand? That is my only name, Vinny!' "

"You told them that? You said 'no way'?"

"Was that good, what I told them, Felita?"

"You did great! Vinny, you're learning fast. It just proves how smart you are and what a bunch of 'bimbos' they all are."

"Don't worry, Felita. When I get real good at speaking English, I'll tell them a lot more. Listen, I'm real happy to be taking these lessons with you."

After our lesson Mami walked in, acting real friendly, and asked us to come into the kitchen. She had set out two tall glasses of milk and two plates of her homemade bread pudding.

"You two have been working hard. I thought that before Vinny goes home he'd like a little bit of bread pudding. It's Puerto Rican style. I make it with brown sugar. I hope you like it, Vinny."

Mami makes the best bread pudding in the world. This was a treat all right. Usually we only got to eat it on Sundays. She asked him all about school and our lessons.

"Mrs. Maldonado, Felita is a fine teacher, and I am very grateful that you allow her to help me," he said.

"Well, you two just keep up the good work," she said. Now I knew she really liked him. When I walked Vinny to the door and we said good-bye, we exchanged glances, knowing we were both relieved that Mami approved of our lessons.

Our lessons were going so good that Vinny asked that during his part of the lesson we only speak in English. Even though he still had a Spanish accent, he hardly made any bad mistakes. But still he asked me so many questions about English that he practically made me dizzy. For example, he wanted to know the meaning of "far out," and no matter how hard I tried to explain it, he couldn't seem to get it.

"It means something good, yes, Felita? Like you win a race in the fastest time. Right?"

"Not exactly, Vinny. It just has to be something unexpected. Like, imagine if you got a new pair of real racing skates that the other kids have never even seen except on T.V. in the roller derby. My brother Tito got himself a pair and when he skates, doing all kinds of great tricks that you never see other kids do, people say, 'Far out!' Now do you understand?"

"Ah ha! Yes, Felita. Listen, for example, when I am learning and talking English so good, soon the kids in school will be telling me, 'Vinny, far out!' Is correct?"

"You got it!" I held out my hand palm up and Vinny slapped it.

"All right!" he shouted. This was something he saw the other boys do and now we practiced it all the time.

My Spanish was coming along pretty good except that Vinny's Colombian accent confused me when I was pronouncing words in Spanish. When I told him that, Vinny just laughed and began speaking Spanish more like me.

"I'm telling you, Felita, not only am I going to talk

in English like you, but when I speak Spanish, I'm going to sound exactly like a Puerto Rican!"

Vinny was real pleased with my progress. He said that now I was speaking and understanding a lot better. When I got to Puerto Rico, he was sure I would have no problems with Spanish. I wished I could be as sure. Before I started taking lessons with Vinny, I never even thought about speaking Spanish all that good. I felt the same way as my brothers, like I'd get by. But now I was beginning to worry a little. After all, I was gonna be there the whole summer; I wasn't leaving after two weeks, like them.

I had kept my promise and didn't tell any of the kids at school about our lessons, except for Gigi. I had to tell her, since we always told each other everything. But I still hadn't told her how I really felt about Vinny. Somehow I couldn't talk about these feelings . . . not even to Gigi. I mean, what if Vinny didn't like me in the same way? I'd really look stupid.

So far me and Vinny had made believe that we really didn't know each other very well when we were in school. And even though I enjoyed this special secret between the two of us, I was getting real anxious to tell my friends about it. Finally, after over a month of lessons, Vinny's English was so much better that we both agreed next week I could tell everyone about our private lessons.

"I don't believe you, Felita," Vivian was saying. "I'll bet you are making the whole thing up!"

"No, she's not either!" Gigi backed me up. "It's all true. Vinny and Felita have been having lessons now for over a whole month. Right?" Gi looked at me.

"Right, but you all don't have to believe me, because when Vinny gets here, I can prove it's all true. He's having lunch with us today. I asked him to come over and eat with us."

"Wow. Far out!" said Elba. "But how come you never said anything before to us?"

"Because we wanted to wait and see if the lessons worked out good. They have and so now you all know."

"How's he doing with his English?" asked Lydia.

"He's speaking much better now, but you can see for yourselves." I waved to Vinny, who was heading toward us with his lunch tray. It was great to see the expressions on everybody's faces. For once Vivian's mouth opened real wide and not a word came out.

"Here, Vinny." Gigi, who was sitting right across the way from me, slid over so that Vinny could sit down.

"Hi, how is everybody?" Vinny made sure he greeted everyone. One thing I was finding out about Vinny Davila, he sure was polite. "Did you get your mother's permission to meet at my house?" he asked me.

"Yes, she said that next week we can meet at your house and see how that works out."

"Great!" Vinny grinned, looking real pleased. "Felita has told you all how she's been helping me to speak in English, yes?"

"Oh, yeah," said Consuela, "and I think that's terrific. You sound real better already."

"You sure do," Elba added. "In fact you are sounding more like one of us."

"Thank you. I feel is an improvement too. That's because Felita is such a good teacher."

"I'll bet she is"—Vivian leaned over toward Vinny

—"but I'm sure you're very good at giving lessons too." She put a stupid smirk on her face when she spoke to me. "How's your Spanish, Felita? Improving too, I'll bet."

"Yes, it is," I said wondering what she was up to.

"Excellent." I saw Vivian wink at Lydia and Elba. "You know I never would have guessed that you two were so close." I could feel myself blushing. What was she trying to say, anyway?

Vivian smiled sweetly at Vinny and then stood up. "Well, I gotta go. I have to check up on something in the library. You coming, Lydia?" Lydia stood and followed Vivian. When they were only a short distance away, Vivian turned around and said loudly, "Good luck with your lessons, Felita and Vinny. I sure hope you both learn a whole lot of good things together!"

That Vivian always has to have the last word! I could feel myself burning up with embarrassment. But when I looked up at Vinny, he was eating calmly. I just hoped he didn't get what I thought she was trying to say.

Later that night as I lay in bed, trying to study the grammar in my Spanish reader, all I could think of was Vinny. When Vivian had made her nasty remarks that afternoon, I was embarrassed because I liked Vinny so much. Lately even my trip to Puerto Rico had seemed less important than being with him. In fact I could hardly wait for Mondays and Thursdays so we could have our lessons and be together. I was getting to like him as much as I liked Gigi, only it was different. When I am with Gigi, I feel secure and happy because I know I can share all my secrets with her, and she will always understand. With Vinny, I get this feeling of excitement like I wanna put my arms around him and give him a big hug. Just looking at the way he laughs or puts his head over to one side makes me feel great. We don't even have to talk! Sometimes just being in the same room with him makes me feel delirious with joy! But I'm also worried. What if he doesn't feel the same way?

How I wished my grandmother was alive so I could talk to her. I just couldn't help wondering why my getting older had to make things so complicated. When I was little, life was a lot simpler. But now my brothers were in charge of me. Mami watched me like I was the gold in Fort Knox and someone was gonna steal me! Plus I knew now that I wanted Vinny to be my boyfriend. Was this wrong?

Mami would never understand. But my abuelita would have, and she would have told me what to do. She would help me and together we could figure all this out. Why, oh, why did she have to die? Why couldn't it have been Tio Jorge instead of her? Right after I thought this, I felt guilty and I spoke out loud. "Forgive me, Abuelita, I really didn't mean it. I know how much you love Tio and I love him too, honest. It's only that right now I'm so confused and I miss

you something fierce." Tears came to my eyes because really I didn't want Tio to die. I know how
much he loves all of us. All I wanted was for Abuelita
to come back to me.

The only person I could talk to was Gigi. So I
decided to feel her out, introduce the subject and see
what she thought. Maybe she could tell me if what I
felt was right, if I had a chance with Vinny or was
way off base. No matter what, I knew I could trust
her.

That next Saturday when Gigi and me sat in her
room, listening to her cassette player, I brought up
the subject of Vinny, trying to sound real casual.

"Gi, do you think Vinny likes Vivian?"

"What? Are you crazy? He doesn't even look her
way."

"Oh, I thought maybe you had observed something about him that I didn't."

"What I observed about Vinny Davila ain't got
nothing to do with Vivian."

"You mean he might like someone else?" I asked.

"He sure does."

I turned my eyes away from Gigi. "Who do you
think she is?"

"Come on, Felita"—Gigi caught my eye and smiled
—"don't be telling me you don't know."

"I don't!" I kept on pretending I didn't know what
she meant.

"You know he likes you. Admit it, Felita. And you

like him too." That's all I wanted to hear. I couldn't keep a straight face anymore.

"Oh, Gigi, you're right. I'm really crazy about him. I just hope he likes me the same way."

"I think you will be Vinny's girl. And it's gonna happen soon."

"Wow. I hope so. If he asks me to be his girl, he's getting a loud YES!" We hugged. I could tell Gigi was real happy for me. "There's only one big problem if that happens, though, and that's Mami. If she knew how I felt about Vinny, she'd kill me and stop the lessons for sure."

"So just make sure she doesn't find out. Act real cool, and don't say a word to her."

"I guess so. You know what really burns me up? My brothers can get away with murder and nobody says anything to them. For instance, Tito can come in the house and say that some girl has fine legs, or is really built, and my parents just laugh. Like it's all so funny, right? Me, I wouldn't dare say a word about Vinny. They say I'm wrong to feel I should be treated like my brothers. Gi, do you think I'm wrong to feel like that?"

"No, you're absolutely right, Felita. You should be equal to your brothers. You're even smarter than them. They can't draw like you, right? Why should boys get more privileges than girls just because they are boys? Doris told me that if I had a brother, we'd be treated the same."

"You're so lucky, Gigi. I wish Mami could be like Doris. It's not that I don't love Mami, because I know she does care for me, but I never can talk to her. She doesn't believe I have problems. I mean it! She thinks I have this perfect life."

"I know I'm lucky because Doris doesn't treat me like most P.R. mothers treat their daughters. She's more modern."

"Even a lot of black girls have it easier too. Look at Elba Thomas. She can go out after school, and lately everybody knows she and Eddie Lopez are seeing each other. It's not some big deep secret. I think the Anglo girls got it the best. Remember when I was friendly with Lynne Coleby last year? Her parents are from here, but her grandparents are from someplace in Europe. Anyway, she can go out anytime, anytime at all, just so long as she tells her mother where she is. When I was hanging out with her, Mami didn't like it. Whenever Lynne came over to visit, Mami would start.

" 'Why doesn't she telephone first to find out if you are free to play outside?'—or—'Don't her parents care how long she stays visiting you?'—and—'I don't believe in them customs, I'm sorry.'

"Mami got on my case so bad, I had to stop seeing her. Mami only likes me to hang out with girls who are kept real strict. She loves me to be with Consuela. Although she does like you a lot, but that's because we've been tight for so many years."

"Don't worry, Felita. When you grow up, you can go to art college and do what you want. Your parents won't be able to tell you what to do and your brothers won't boss you. Besides, soon you're going to P.R. to spend the whole summer with your Tio Jorge. No parents or brothers, right?"

"All right!" I felt much better already.

"When are you going over to Vinny's house?" asked Gigi.

"Monday. I hope you're right about what you said." I was feeling so excited at the idea of being Vinny's girl that I could hardly sit still.

"Don't worry, Felita, I'm right. You'll see."

The following Monday I was getting ready to go over to Vinny's house when Mami spoke to me. "Felita, Johnny will be taking you over to Vinny's house."

"What?" I was furious. "Why, Mami? I don't need no baby-sitter. Vinny only lives down the block, like two minutes away!"

"Because you are too young to go alone to a stranger's house and—"

"Stranger?" I interrupted her. "What do you mean? Vinny's been coming here now for over a month! And we see each other every day in school."

"Just you listen to me, chica." When Mami folds her hands and stands in a certain way with her back arched, I just know she means serious business. "It is not proper for a girl soon to become a woman to be going to a boy's house unescorted. The Davila family are from another country and a Latino culture so they will see this as wrong. Do you understand me?"

"Vinny comes here without an escort."

"That's right! He's un hombrecito, a young man. You are a young woman. No one will talk about him, but everyone will talk about you." I looked at my mother and wanted to say who cares? But I knew better. If I got her too angry, she might stop the lessons.

"Will Johnny have to take me there again on Thursday?"

"Yes."

"And the next time?"

"Sí señorita, very definitely."

"For God's sake, Mami. This is so embarrassing! Just how long does Johnny have to keep taking me there?"

"For as long as you keep going and I say so." I was so annoyed at Mami that I slammed down my books and sank into the armchair. "There is, of course, another solution." Mami paused. "You don't go at all."

"Thanks a lot!" I snapped.

"Don't you get sarcastic with me. Just consider yourself lucky that I'm even letting you go there." I just nodded. Like what choice did I have?

As we went over to Vinny's building, Johnny

rushed along so fast I could barely keep up with him.

"Hey, man, slow down! Where's the fire?"

"Look, Felita, I don't like doing this any more than you do. Taking you over to some people's house I don't even know is not my idea of a great afternoon."

"So why don't you say no for once to Mami, and do us both a favor?"

"Sure, right away. You know I can't."

"You can't or you won't?"

"I can't and you know it too. Now get off my back!" I sulked, practically running to keep up with him. But I had to admit that Johnny was right. If he said no to Mami, she'd tell my father. Then Johnny might be grounded for days or punished in some other way.

"You don't have to stick around during the lesson . . . I hope, do you?" I asked nervously.

"No, thank God. But I gotta come back later on and pick you up."

"Hey, look, I'm sorry, Johnny." I really did feel sorry for him. He was nice to me most of the time and very rarely raised his voice. "Truce?" I smiled up at him.

"Sure," he said, putting his arm around my shoulder. "I know it's not your fault either." I felt better knowing we weren't still angry at each other.

After climbing four long flights, we finally caught our breath in front of a door with the nameplate

Davila. Vinny welcomed us with a big smile. Speaking in Spanish, he introduced us to his mother and a bunch of little kids who were laughing and running around in the narrow foyer. "And this is Maritza, my sister, my brothers Julio and David, and the terror of our house, baby Iris." They all had the same coloring and freckles as Vinny.

"Hello, everybody!" baby Iris said in English, surprising everyone. She was real cute and only around three years old.

"Iris is a big showoff." Mrs. Davila laughed and led us into the living room. Their apartment was smaller than ours. There were different flower patterns everywhere: on the linoleum, on the curtains, even on the upholstery. The walls were filled with framed colorful embroideries and small rugs. Next to a large color T.V. there was a tiny altar set up with plastic flowers, religious pictures, and a lighted red candle.

Mrs. Davila handed my brother a big plastic bowl and spoke to him in Spanish. "This is for your mother. It's a dessert we call arequipe. It's the most famous dessert in my country. Tell her it's a milk and sugar pudding."

After Johnny left, Vinny and I followed Mrs. Davila into the kitchen. "I've cleared a place on the table here where you two can work. Have a good and productive lesson."

There were two little yellow-and-brown songbirds

in a bright green cage. "Oh, how sweet," I said. "My grandmother used to have a parakeet. His name was Pepito. After she died, he only lived for a short time. I think what happened was that Pepito missed her. Actually, this whole apartment reminds me of my abuelita's house."

"My parents like to have things around that remind them of home, like all those rugs and embroideries."

"Why did your family come here, Vinny?"

"Well . . ." I could see that Vinny looked uncomfortable and I wished I hadn't asked him that question.

"Look, I'm sorry. You don't have to answer me."

"That's all right, Felita. It's just that back home even though there are a lot of good things, it's also hard to live. Like to find work is hard. My father says back home there are too many people and not enough jobs. Most of my friends there never finish school. They have to quit and go to work. My parents wanted something better for us."

"I'm sorry, Vinny."

"It's all right, Felita. Sometimes I do think about home and I miss a lot of things there—the great weather, my friends, all my relatives. Felita, for you, it's different, you were born here. But for me, it's not the same."

"I think I know what you mean because my grandmother missed her home too, even though she lived here for many, many years. She used to talk to me about Puerto Rico all the time."

We worked on my Spanish for most of the lesson. But what made me feel really good was that even though Vinny hadn't said anything about being his girl yet, I knew we were becoming better friends. I figured sooner or later he would ask me. I only hoped it would be sooner.

Things started to look even better the following week when Vinny began to wait for me after school. We walked home with Consuela and Joanie. It was nice and warm out these days, and it stayed light longer. Yes, spring was definitely here.

Ever since Vinny and I started having lessons, my brothers seemed to be less on my back. Johnny was never a real bad problem, but Tito really surprised me. Although he wasn't my bosom pal, he had stopped being so nasty and hardly ever teased me. In fact he was actually nice. Like earlier this afternoon when I came home from school, Vinny and me were downstairs, standing by the stoop, and Tito came along. Usually he'd say something mean and send me upstairs, but this time he stopped, said hello, and even asked Vinny how things were going. I couldn't believe my eyes or my ears as I listened.

"How are you doing, man? How's the lessons going? You learning some English?"

"Yes, thank you, Tito. I think I'm doing good.

Felita is the teacher and she says I'm passing my grade."

"Excellent! Vinny, why don't you come on down to the playground sometimes, like after school or on the weekend, and play some ball? There's a bunch of guys there about your age. I'll introduce you around."

"That's great! Thank you a lot, Tito."

"No sweat. See you guys."

And then he left without saying another word. Now I was waiting for Tito to get home so I could thank him. I heard him come in and waited a few minutes, then I went over to his room and knocked on the door.

"Come in."

"Hi, Tito. Where's Johnny?"

"I don't know, still out, I guess. What's up?"

"Well, I just wanted to thank you for being so nice to Vinny."

"Oh, sure," said Tito. "Well, he's a nice kid and I figured he's shy on account of his problems with English, so I'd show him around. No sweat."

"Vinny was real pleased. He's so nice, Tito."

"You like him, don't you?" Tito smiled.

"Of course I like him"—I was trying not to blush —"he's my friend."

"Hey, Felita, it's okay if you two like each other." I looked at Tito, surprised that he knew how I felt. "I know you like him, Felita."

"You do?" I sat down on his bunk bed.

"Sure."

"Are you going to tell Mami?"

"Why should I tell Mami?"

"Because she's always sending you out to check up on me or to watch over me. You know what I'm saying, Tito."

"Look, Felita, what you do is your business as far as I'm concerned. In fact, if you wanna know the truth, it is a pain in my butt to have to be in charge of you. And always to be listening to Mami and Papi telling me how good you are, what a great student you are, and how special you are because you happen to be a girl. Making me out like some stupid slob that can't do nothing right. And you wanna know something else? Until you started seeing Vinny and I saw that you liked him and was trying to keep it from Mami, I thought you could never do anything except what our parents wanted you to do. Like little Miss Perfect, you know? Now I admire you for doing what you want, whether Mami likes it or not. I mean, as long as you don't do nothing bad, what's the difference?"

I was really surprised at what Tito was saying. I mean he's usually so smug and sure of himself. "I didn't know you felt like that. I don't think you're stupid. You're so great at skating and sports, and you always make such great jokes and make everybody laugh. And anyway, I sure ain't perfect. I always thought you just didn't like me."

"I like you, Felita. It's just that it pisses me off sometimes when you get all kinds of privileges, like your own room, and now going to P.R. for the whole summer. Johnny and me don't get none of that. And sometimes I have to come home early in the middle of a game just to be looking out for you."

"Oh, yeah? Well, at least you get to go out anytime you want, Tito. Nobody keeps tabs on you. I can't go nowhere or see anybody unless Mami lets me. Sometimes I feel like I'm in jail. It's really a drag, you know? That's what being a girl means in this house. You wanna trade places? You wouldn't like it and you know it too!"

"I guess I wouldn't." We looked at each other and both of us smiled. "Look, Felita, your secret is safe with me."

"Thanks, Tito." I wanted to tell him that I didn't even know if Vinny liked me and that there might not be any secret to keep. But I also liked the idea that Tito thought that Vinny was my boyfriend. I was feeling happy and close to my brother and I didn't want to change things by saying anything more. I stood up. "I'm glad we talked, Tito. Listen, anytime you need a favor, you know who to come to."

"Sure. Thanks, Felita."

When I got back to my room, I realized that this

was the first time I had really seen my brother as a kid with problems too, and someone I was beginning to like.

The next Thursday, after lunch, we were all allowed to spend some time out in the school yard. Kids were playing different games—basketball, hopscotch, jump rope—or just hanging out. We all picked a spot by the school fence where it was warm and sunny. We were busy talking when I heard someone calling me and whistling.

"Felita . . . hey! Yoo hoo, Felita!" It was Joey, Eddie, the twins Dan and Duane, and Paquito. They walked over to us.

"Buenos dias, Señorita Felita . . ." Joey bowed real low. "Would you all like me, José Ramos, to teech you Spaneesh privately, my deeer?" I knew he was putting on a Spanish accent, trying to imitate Vinny. "And you can teech me Eeenglish!" That fool was shouting so loud that some other kids came over and began to laugh. I couldn't believe that Joey could be so evil.

"Get out of here, you idiot!" I went right over to him, ready to smack him right in his ugly grinning face.

"Just cut it out, you guys!" Gigi was yelling at them. I walked up to Joey, but he just backed away like a coward.

"Hey, man, what's the matter with you, Felita?"

That Joey just wouldn't stop. "Ain't you happy to be Señor Beenie's señorita?" Then all Joey's dumbo friends started making kissing sounds at me while they kept on following him like a bunch of fools, laughing at every silly thing he said.

"Look, stupid Joey Ramos, I ain't nobody's señorita, so why don't you quit sitting on your brains! Moron!" Finally they all turned around and took off.

"Gross," said Consuela. "Don't you pay them no mind, Felita."

"They are just too dumb." Gigi put her arm around me.

"Well," Lydia said, "you gotta admit that you and Vinny spend a lot of time together."

"Yeah, and it looks to everyone like he's your boyfriend." Naturally Vivian had to put in her two cents.

"No, Vivian, not to everyone. Only to the imbeciles. Vinny happens to be my good friend, and besides, it ain't nobody's business, you know."

"Excuse me." Vivian turned and began to walk off.

"You are excused all right!" I made sure she heard me. Of course Lydia took off after her.

"I think we should change the subject," said Elba.

"Since I don't care what anybody thinks, I think you are right." Before I could say another word, the school bell rang and we all went back to class.

After school Vinny, Consuela, and Joanie and me were walking home when we saw Joey and the other boys across the street. They began calling out to us.

"Hey, Felita and Vinny! Love is such a wonderful thing!" Then they begin to make all kinds of smacking and kissing noises, waving their arms and jumping around like a bunch of monkeys. I became so embarrassed that I could feel myself burning up with anger. In fact I was so self-conscious, I couldn't say one word.

"Just don't pay attention, Felita," said Vinny. "Soon they will get tired and stop. They only want to make us angry because they are jealous." We just kept going, ignoring them, until finally they headed in another direction. We walked along not saying much until we reached the big intersection where Consuela and Joanie leave us.

"Felita, I'll see you next week during Easter vacation," Consuela said. "You're coming out to play, right?"

"Sure, especially now that the weather's so great. Hope you can come over to my house."

"I'll ask my mother, but you know who's gotta come with me." She pointed to Joanie. "I can't get rid of her."

"That's cause she loves her little sister so much," said Joanie, sticking out her tongue and crossing her eyes. That Joanie could be real cute sometimes.

Vinny and I went on walking down the block. We weren't going to have a lesson today, or any lessons during Easter vacation either. Mami had decided there was too much shopping to do for Easter Sunday, and too much work to do at home during Easter week. When I told Vinny, I could see he was disappointed.

"I'm gonna miss our lessons," he said.

"Me too. But we'll be getting right back to work after vacation."

"That's right! I hope to see you outdoors, Felita."

"That would be great. I know I'll be coming out, probably every day." We stopped in front of my building.

"Have a nice Easter, Felita."

"Maybe I'll see you in church on Easter Sunday, Vinny. Are you all coming to the Spanish Mass?"

"Yes, we'll be there."

"See you!"

"See you soon, Felita." As Vinny waved and walked toward his building, I felt that Sunday couldn't get here fast enough for me!

On Easter Sunday me and my whole family got dressed up in our new Easter outfits. We were heading toward St. Joseph's Church to attend the twelve o'clock Mass because it was going to be read in Spanish. Most of the Catholics in our neighborhood go to St. Joseph's. That's where my brothers and I made our communion and confirmation. The streets were filled with people on their way to church in their brand-new clothes. Even Doña Josefina, who usually opens up her bodega for half a day on Sundays, had closed her store. She was all sharped up, wearing a big lavender hat with green and white flowers all over it. Just about all the shops on my street were closed, including the candy-and-stationery store where people buy their Sunday papers.

I was praying that Vinny would be at church. I wanted him to see how good I looked. This year I had grown so much that we had to shop in the Junior Miss section. Mami had let me choose my own clothes without too much of a fuss, and this morning she'd even let me put on some pink lipstick and a little bit of eye shadow. I was wearing a real pretty off-white suit with a bright blue turtleneck blouse. I'd looked at myself in the mirror before we'd left and I liked what I saw .

When we got to church, it was real crowded. I saw Consuela and her family, Gigi and Doris, Lydia, Vivian, and a whole bunch of other kids, but not Vinny. Papi led us toward the far side of the church, over to an empty pew. As we sat down I heard some little kids giggling. When I turned around, I saw Maritza, Julio, David, and baby Iris all waving at me. Vinny was sitting next to his parents and gave me a big smile.

"Hey, there's Vinny," Tito whispered.

"I know." My heart was beating so loud I could hardly hear what the priest was saying. After Mass I spoke to my parents. "Did you see the Davila family? Why don't we go and say hello." I was looking for any excuse to talk to Vinny.

When we walked over to them, Mrs. Davila was all smiles in Johnny's direction. "I know this young man very well. He's a good and responsible brother who takes good care of his sister." I wished she hadn't said that, because right away Mami takes off on one of her speeches.

"Indeed, Mrs. Davila. I want you to understand that our Felita is not allowed to run around wildly, as is the custom in this country." I couldn't wait for Mami to shut up. I felt so embarrassed that I wanted to fall right through the cracks in the sidewalk. But even though I felt like I was burning up inside, I tried to act real calm. When I looked at Vinny, he smiled so sweetly at me that I knew he was on my side. It made me feel a whole lot better.

Later my parents took us all to a movie and then we had dinner out. That was a real treat because my folks had been saving every cent for our trip to Puerto Rico, and nowadays we never ate out.

The rest of our Easter vacation turned out to be just wonderful. Gigi came over to my house almost every day. It didn't rain once and the weather was nice and warm, so that everyone played outdoors. Even Vinny's brothers and sisters began playing outdoors with some other little kids. Vinny played a lot of softball with the other boys in the park. We'd go there and watch the boys, or just hang out and play our games. Mostly us girls jumped rope, or played hopscotch and jacks. When we played tag with the boys, everyone noticed how Vinny was always catching me.

"Hey, man, Vinny," yelled Eddie Lopez, "why don't you catch somebody else for a change? There's other people in this game, you know!"

I didn't even mind the teasing just as long as I could be with Vinny every day. Once when we were all playing hide-and-go-seek on our block, it was Vinny's turn to be it. This time instead of hiding with somebody else, I took off down the street and hid in an alleyway all by myself. When Vinny found me, he bent over and gave me a long kiss right on the mouth. Then he smiled and said, "You're it, Felita!"

I was so shocked that I stayed perfectly still. I couldn't even move. Nobody had ever kissed me like that before. I mean of course I had kissed boys before, like at Lydia's birthday party when we had to play spin the bottle. But I didn't like any of those boys and thought the whole thing was just sloppy.

"Felita, you're it!" I heard all my friends shouting. "Come out, come out, wherever you are!" I recognized Consuela's voice.

When I finally got back to the game, I felt like I was walking on air and my insides were dancing all by themselves. Even though Vinny still hadn't asked me to be his girl, now I knew that we liked each other in a way that no one else could understand.

The month of May seemed to go by real fast. Final term tests were due just before graduation. Next year our class was going on to junior high school. Everyone was trying to study extra hard, since no one wanted to stay back. Mami decided that from now until June, Vinny and I should meet for only one lesson a week, on Wednesdays. I wasn't very happy about it and neither was Vinny. But we did have a lot of schoolwork to get through and this time we both admitted Mami was right. Besides, I was doing extra work on a project with Mrs. Feller, the librarian. We were making a large paper banner painted with our school colors—navy blue and gold. It said:

CONGRATULATIONS TO THE GRADUATES OF P.S. 47
WE ARE THE BEST

We were also making a huge autograph album to be used on stage during the ceremonies. It was five feet high and four feet wide. We used papier-mâché and paint to make it look like it was real leather. On the album cover I made a drawing of our school building and underneath I painted the words PLEASE SIGN ME. On the inside cover I painted: NAMES OF GRADUATES. Kids could sign their names underneath. I worked almost every day on this project so that we could have it ready for graduation. I had two other kids as helpers, but Mrs. Feller and I did most of the work.

When I wasn't staying after school to work on the album, Vinny walked me home. I also got to see him on Wednesdays for our lesson. Mami was frantic with her shopping and preparing for our trip. I was glad too, because that way she had too much to do to be keeping tabs on me. Vinny and I had already had our last lesson two days ago. Today we decided that we would walk the long way home from school so that we could say good-bye by ourselves without Mami being around.

We decided to stop at a small park that was far enough from school and our block so that we wouldn't bump into anyone we knew. Except for some older people feeding the pigeons, no one was around. We sat on a bench all by ourselves.

"July Second is when we all go to P.R., Vinny. That's not very far away."

"I know. But think, Felita, you're going to have a wonderful time there."

"I guess," I said. But I was almost wishing I didn't have to leave; things were going so good here. "I wish both you and Gigi could come with us. You two are my very best friends."

"I'm gonna miss you so much, Felita."

"You are?" I was so pleased to hear him say that.

"Yes, and I hope you don't forget me."

"Forget you, Vinny? You gotta be crazy!"

"Then promise that you'll write to me."

"I promise," I said. "Will you write back?"

"I promise, if you promise me one thing. . . ."

"Anything," I told him.

Vinny put his arm around my shoulders, then leaned toward me and kissed me right on the mouth. This time it wasn't such a surprise, and when he finished, I kissed him right back. "Will you still be my girlfriend when you get back from Puerto Rico?" he asked.

My heart seemed to jump right into my throat. Up until that moment Vinny had never actually said I was his girl. "Yes, you know I will," I told him.

I managed to get pretty good marks on all my tests except math. That's always been one of my worst subjects. I wish I had Consuela's brains for math. She's a whiz at it. At last graduation day came, and it was a great big success. Everybody kept admiring the decorations and the big album. I even got a special mention for my artwork and had to stand up and take a bow. Everyone clapped, and even though I was real nervous, I loved it. Mami, Tio Jorge, and Johnny were there, but Papi had to work and Tito had school.

Toward the end of the ceremonies Mrs. Feller told the whole graduating class to come up on stage and sign their names with Magic Markers in the big album. I had already signed my name first. Then we all began to say good-bye. Some of the kids were crying. They were sad because not all of us were going to the same junior high. Most of the kids lived in our district, but some others who lived in other areas had to go to a different junior high. For instance, Gigi and I weren't going to the same school. That really upset us both because we'd never been separated since we had started school together. But Consuela and most of the other girls would be going to my school and so would Vinny, so I couldn't stay too sad. When I said good-bye to Vinny again, he squeezed my hand and whispered to me not to forget to write.

That evening Mami cooked a delicious celebration dinner. Papi was home and all of us were real excited about our trip. Tio bought me a vanilla cake with pineapple icing that had been decorated with the words

BUENA SUERTE

GOOD LUCK

FELITA!

Except for my parents, none of us had ever been up on an airplane before. Tio Jorge was the most nervous. "Birds are supposed to fly, not people. I don't like it," he grumbled the morning we were leaving.

"Por Dios, Tio," Mami said, "it's nothing. You're gonna feel like you are standing still. When I first came here from Puerto Rico twenty years ago, it was nothing; imagine today when things are so modern. Tell him please, Alberto."

"Rosa is right, Tio Jorge, you have nothing to worry about. I guarantee it," said Papi. "You will feel like you are sitting in the living room and not up in the sky." Papi had been a mechanic in the air force before he married Mami, so everyone knew he was telling the truth.

"It's not natural . . . I don't like it," Tio kept on complaining.

"I can't wait to go, man," said Tito. "You should've seen my buddies, man, green with envy."

Mami went around the apartment double-checking to make sure the windows were locked and all the appliances were unplugged. "We are not coming back for two weeks," she said, "so everyone make sure they got all their things packed away."

The buzzer sounded from downstairs and we all filed out of our apartment. Chuco, my father's friend from work, was driving us to the airport in his car.

When we got to the airport, I felt so excited, because even though I've been there before, it's always been to greet somebody coming in or say good-bye to somebody going out. Now it was my turn to travel.

On the plane I got a window seat next to my parents. Tio sat next to Tito and Johnny in another window seat. They sat directly in front of us. When the engines started and the plane took off, I got so scared I held on to Mami's arm with both hands.

"It's gonna be all right, Felita. In a moment we will be high up and you won't even feel like you are moving." She was right. After a while all the buildings and water down below disappeared and all I could see outside was a white fog. The plane felt like it was standing still. When the drink cart came around, I ordered a ginger ale and the flight attendant put a cherry in it for me. Later we had lunch. The food looked a whole lot better than it tasted. Still, it was fun to get my very own tray. It made me feel like a grown-up. I got up and walked around, but there wasn't any place to go to. I saw that Tio Jorge was sleeping. My brothers were reading sports magazines and listening to music on the headphones. I went back to my seat, put the headphones on too, and before I knew it I fell asleep. Mami woke me to tell me that we were going to land in San Juan in a few minutes.

"Look, Felita," Mami said. "There are palm trees!" When the plane landed, all the passengers applauded. We got our luggage and went toward the exit. In the airport lots of people were waving and calling out names in Spanish. We heard somebody call out our names. From the pictures we had at home I recognized my mother's sister, Aunt Julia, and her brother, Uncle Tomás. They came running over with Mami's father, Abuelo Juan, followed by two little kids, a boy around nine and a girl around seven, as well as two older boys around my brothers' ages. I knew from the pictures at home that they were my cousins: Carlito, his little sister Lina, and José and his brother Tony. Mami and Aunt Julia began to cry, but it was Abuelo Juan who was crying the loudest.

"At last!" he said, wiping his eyes and blowing

his nose, "I've seen my daughter and my grand-children. I'm content now and ready to meet my maker anytime." Abuelo stepped back and looked carefully at me and my brothers. "Now, do you children understand your grandfather? Do you understand Spanish?" We all said yes. "Very good," he said in English and laughed. "I know a little English too, listen: 'How much it costs, please? Sorry, is too much money!'" Everyone laughed with Abuelo. Then Uncle Tomás picked Mami up and spun her around.

"Rosita, you look as beautiful as ever!" I noticed that Aunt Julia, Uncle Tomás, and Mami all had dark complexions like Abuelo Juan as well as his same smile.

We split up into two cars. It was very hot and the sun was so strong that I had to squint to see clearly. But once we got into my uncle's car, he put on the air conditioner and it got cool and comfortable. All through the ride to Abuelo Juan's, Lina kept on holding and squeezing my hand.

"Felita," said Uncle Tomás, "ever since Lina heard you were coming here, she has talked of nothing else. Every day she asked us, 'When is my cousin, Felita, coming from New York?'"

"That's right"—Lina hugged me—"you are going to be my very best friend, right?"

"Sure"—I looked over at Carlito—"and your brother's friend too."

Lina whispered in my ear, "You don't wanna be his friend, all he's interested in is sports."

"Here we are." Uncle Tomás pulled up in front of a house painted bright green with white and yellow trimming. I noticed that all the houses in the neighborhood were painted in two or three colors and had lots of flower pots on the porches. Inside Abuelo Juan's house a chubby old lady wearing a large apron came over and started hugging everybody.

"Just call me Abuela Angelina, or plain Abuela. I know I cannot take the place of your real grandmother, who is now in heaven"—Abuela Angelina made the sign of the cross—"may she rest in peace. But I am your other grandmother now, and I love you all because we are family."

"Angelina is a wonderful cook," Abuelo said proudly. And something sure did smell delicious.

Everybody sat down at a long table. In front of us were large platters filled with yellow rice, red beans, root plants with garlic and olive oil, fried fish, meat, avocado salad, all kinds of vegetables, and fresh bread.

"You can't eat like this where you people come from." Abuelo kept piling food on everybody's plate. "This here is authentic Island food. One hundred percent Puerto Rican!" Everything tasted delicious.

"Papa, I'm going to steal my sister away from you," said Uncle Tomás.

"Oh, no, no sir." Abuelo reached over and hugged

Mami. "I've waited too long to see my daughter and her family, so you will just have to wait your turn." It felt so nice being with all my new family. I knew they were not really new, but since I'd never met them before, it felt that way.

"Rosa, Alberto," Abuelo suddenly said in a serious voice, "how come your children can hardly speak Spanish? Not so much Felita, she does all right. But the way the boys speak is a disgrace! Why didn't you teach them the language of their parents and grandparents? Why?"

Mami looked very upset. "Papa, it's hard to teach the kids Spanish because everyone back in the States speaks English. Two languages would have only confused them. We wanted them to concentrate on their schoolwork, not on speaking Spanish. Besides—"

"Nonsense!" Abuelo interrupted Mami. "It wouldn't have done no harm. Especially if you would have taught them in the home. I cannot understand how folks can leave here and then forget their language. It's not right! I don't like it!"

Mami sat perfectly still with her head bowed. I could see she was feeling miserable. In fact she reminded me of myself when I got hollered at by her and Papi. I looked over at my brothers, but they kept their eyes lowered too. No one was saying a word and there was dead silence at the table.

Finally Papi said, "Listen, Don Juan, sometimes things happen that we have very little control over, okay? But now we are doing something to remedy the situation. Johnny and Tito are studying Spanish in school and while they are in Puerto Rico, they can learn even more. As for Felita, by the time she gets back home after the summer, she'll be talking Spanish like a parrot."

"Very good!" Abuelo stopped looking angry. "I'm glad, Alberto." He looked at my brothers. "Now you two boys will begin to learn to speak Spanish properly like real Puerto Ricans and not like the gringos. Understand?"

Johnny and Tito looked like they wanted to bolt right out of there. Was I glad for my lessons with Vinny! At least I could speak a whole lot better than my brothers.

That evening I met so many relatives I never even knew I had, like all kinds of cousins, aunts, and uncles. Most of the grown-ups sat out in back talking. I could hear Mami's laugh and Papi's voice coming through all the other voices. The real little kids were inside watching T.V. Lina kept on following me around and babbling nonstop. I was beginning to feel like I was Consuela minding little Joanie.

Most of us kids were hanging out on the front porch. In fact it looked like most of the neighborhood was doing the same. Cars and trucks kept coming down the block so that the kids playing out in the street had to jump back onto the sidewalk. When an ice-cream truck came by and parked by the corner,

Abuelo bought all of us ice cream. As I sat on the steps watching the action, a strange feeling came over me: I felt like I had been here before. Then I realized that in so many ways it was just like I was back on my own street. The traffic, the grown-ups and kids hanging out, and the ice-cream truck were so much like home.

But here everyone spoke Spanish and being outside was real easy. You didn't have to go up and down the stairs or go in and out of big buildings. Also there were so many plants and trees around that it felt and smelled like I was in the park. I thought about all my friends, especially Gigi, Consuela, and Vinny. Right now I bet they were hanging out just like me. How I wished they could all be here with me and see some of this.

Some of the older kids were playing disco on a cassette player. Tito had gotten up and began explaining in his broken Spanish all about break-dancing. I couldn't believe it. He began to give a demonstration. I went over and stood by Johnny, who smiled at me and whispered, "What a show-off that Tito is!" Really, Tito didn't break-dance all that good. Back home they would have laughed him off the street, believe me. But here they didn't know the difference. There were two older girls watching Tito, one around fourteen and the other around sixteen. I could see he really wanted to impress them. When he finished his break-dancing, he walked right up to them and went into real loud rap-talking:

> "I'm from New York City where the girls are fine
> but not so pretty—
> uh huh huh, huh huh!
> Now here in P.R. the girls are
> more beautiful by far!
> uh huh huh, huh huh!
> Hey, you all may think I'm a gringo from the
> way I'm speakin' . . .
> But in point of fact I'm a Puerto Rican. . . ."

Everybody laughed and clapped for Tito. Even though we knew what was happening with our brother, Johnny and me had to admit that sometimes Tito could really be fun.

Early the next morning we all went to visit Old San Juan. We saw a large cathedral, a museum, and an old fortress. Mami and Papi kept on saying how much things had changed. "All these expensive restaurants and boutiques!" Mami was outraged. "We might as well be back in a fancy neighborhood in New York."

I didn't care what they thought, since it was all new to me and I was enjoying myself. That night, though, I realized that Tio Jorge was really upset by all the changes he saw. "I can't imagine my village will have changed as much as the city," he said. "I'm sure everything will be just as I remember it . . . you'll see, Felita."

Tio Jorge was waiting for his belongings to arrive so he could go up to his village. He had been real anxious about his nature collection. "Everything else I can replace, but not my collection, that can never be duplicated," he said. But the next day when his boxes arrived everything was in good condition. Papi drove him up to his village. I was going up there to join Tio with my parents and brothers three days before they had to leave for home.

We spent the rest of the time sightseeing around the Island and meeting all kinds of relatives for the first time. There was only one thing that bothered me, and that was the remarks some people made about our Spanish. "Why don't your children speak Spanish, Rosa?" I was sick to death of that question, but the worst was a couple of times when some of the other kids called us Nuyoricans. One day when we were all at the beach visiting Aunt Julia and Uncle Mario, our cousins José and Tony kept on getting on my brothers' case about the way they mispronounced words in Spanish. We had spread out a blanket and put out the beach chairs. The grown-ups were busy setting up cold drinks and food. José and Tony wouldn't let up.

"So what do you think about the Chicago Cubs this year?" José asked Johnny.

"I don't think they stand a chance," Johnny said in Spanish.

"Why don't you explain what you mean, Johnny? You make a statement then you don't explain yourself," said Tony. I could see that Johnny was getting nervous on account of his having to speak in Spanish.

"Well"—Johnny switched to speaking English—"the way I see it, compared to the Pirates, they don't stand a chance. Especially with the number of games they still got to play before the season ends. You know what I mean?"

José looked at Tony and winked. "No, Johnny, I don't understand what you said. Why can't you tell us in Spanish so we know what you're talking about?"

From like nowhere Tito jumped right in between José and Johnny. "Because he can't, sucker! And *we* can't! Understand? Why don't you try us out in English? I'll bet your English sucks! Go on, say something in English, punk!"

"We are Puerto Ricans," said Tony, coming up to Tito. "That's why. Not Nuyoricans!"

Tito turned and faced Tony. "Well, we are Nuyoricans and proud of it!" he said. Then he leapt up at Tony and pushed him so hard that Tony practically went flying as he fell down on the sand. "Why don't you shove it, freak! Come on, Tony, show me how good you are with your fists instead of your girlie mouth! . . . Show me!"

Tony just lay there looking up at Tito in a state of shock. "You wanna start something, wise-ass?" yelled Tito. "Come on. Get up!" Then Johnny ran over to Tito and pushed him back. "Cut it out, Tito. We ain't supposed to be fighting. Quit it."

"What's happening here?" shouted Papi as all the grown-ups came running over. "Tito, what are you up to now? Are you starting trouble?"

Tony stood up real quick. "It's nothing, Tio Alberto," he said. "We were just playing around, trying out some karate moves, and Tito got the best of me. That's all. Honest."

"José, Tony, are you starting trouble with your cousins?" asked Uncle Mario. All the boys shook their heads. "I don't want to hear that you are fighting with your family. If I hear or see another incident that looks like a fight, it will go badly for both of you, Tony and José."

After the grown-ups left, José spoke first. "Hey you guys, let's go in for a swim. Come on."

Tony went over to my brothers. "Come on, Tito, Johnny, let's have some fun. I got a great surfboard I want you to try." They all left, acting pretty friendly. Of course, nobody invited me to come along, right? I'm only a girl. Man, I never saw such boys! They act like you don't exist. Well, I didn't care. Who wanted to be with a bunch of jerks who fought all the time?

I stood by the shore and watched the waves hit my

feet, then I plunged into the cool water, floated on my back, and looked up at the clear blue sky. In just two days I was going up into the mountains to stay with Tio Jorge. I hadn't given that much thought. Actually I had been having such a good time that I hadn't thought much about anything. But soon my parents and brothers were going home and I would be staying in a place I didn't even know with people I'd never even met. The whole idea made me feel uneasy, and part of me wished I was going home too.

That evening I decided to write to my friends. I sent Consuela a card showing the beach and lots of palm trees and Gigi a card that had four different scenes of Old San Juan. Then since I knew how much Vinny liked adventure stories, I sent him a card showing the old fortress in San Juan complete with cannons. I hoped he still liked me as much as I liked him. I wrote him that as soon as I got settled, I would give him my address. Tomorrow I was gonna mail out the cards. Actually just writing to my friends and remembering them had made me feel better.

When it was time to leave
for Jorge's village, Papi rented a car to drive us there.
We stayed on a superhighway for a long time. "This
highway wasn't here when I was a kid. In fact," Papi
said, "it used to take us about two days instead of
two hours to get to and from San Juan." After a
while all the large factories and apartment buildings
disappeared, and we were in the countryside.

Papi turned off the highway and started up a country road. The flamboyan trees that my abuelita had
always told me about were all in full bloom. The
flowers were such a brilliant red that when the sun
shone on them, it looked like parts of the country-

side were on fire. Papi had to drive slowly because there were so many sharp turns and deep drops in the narrow road that it felt like a rollar coaster ride. All of us were getting a little nervous as we looked over the sides of the steep mountains into the valley far below. There were houses built right on the edge of the road, and when we least expected it, some chickens or goats would come running in front of the car. A couple of times Papi had to swerve the car so that he wouldn't crash into them.

"Now, this still reminds me of my childhood"— Papi was laughing—"all the animals running loose. Look at that rude goat—he doesn't care who gets in his way!"

"Please, Alberto, please be careful!" Mami was getting very upset. "You might hit one of those animals. Watch it!"

"So, we hit an animal, and then what, eh? Rosa, can you still remember how to cook goat stew? Or maybe we can have rice and chicken tonight." I could see that Papi was enjoying himself teasing Mami.

"Stop being so silly, Alberto! Just watch the road before you miss a turn and we all become human hamburgers." We continued to climb higher and higher into the mountains.

"You are being very quiet, Miss Felita," said Papi, "are you okay?"

"Sure." Actually I was feeling kind of sad thinking about how much I was gonna miss everybody.

"Hey, Felita, I got a great idea. Why don't we change places?" Tito asked, as if he had read my mind. "This way I'll stay here and you can go back home."

"Never mind, Tito." I wasn't all *that* sad.

"See?" Tito grinned at me. "You know a good thing when you see it, girl!"

"Felita, you are gonna have a wonderful summer," said Mami. "And it will also be good for Tio to have you here. This way he won't be so lonely without the family."

"Besides, didn't we all have a good time this trip? What do you kids say?"

"Terrific time, Papi," Johnny said.

"Great," said Tito. "In fact I'd like to stay away longer. I'm serious. I met me some nice people. Man, I never knew we had so many relatives! Only one thing that I didn't like, and that's the way some of them got on our case about speaking Spanish. I really didn't like José and Tony calling us Nuyoricans and acting like we were ignorant or something."

"Yeah," agreed Johnny, "they kept on correcting me until it got on my nerves. They only called me gringito once, though, because I really told them to shove it!"

"All right!" Tito said. "And I told them, 'Look, if I'm a Nuyorican from New York, then what happens if somebody comes from Chicago, or Boston or Philadelphia? Are they Chicagoricans or Bostonricans or Phillyricans, or what? Because if so, you're all nothing but a bunch of dumbricans born in P.R.' " Even Mami and Papi had to laugh this time. "Man, I can't wait for that José and Tony to visit us at home, because me and Johnny are gonna get on their case about the way they speak English. Like watch out! We'll fix em! Right, bro?"

"Right!" Johnny slapped Tito's open palm.

"You will not do any such thing," Mami said. "I won't have it."

Tito, who was sitting next to me, gave me a poke. "Oh, sure, Mami, we will treat them just like the sweet little gentlemens they are."

"Never mind your nonsense, Tito. Maybe now when you and your brother get back to school, you'll take your Spanish more seriously," said Mami.

"Do you boys think you learned how to speak Spanish a little better than before you got here?" Papi asked.

"No, I didn't learn how to speak any better because they all made me feel too self-conscious. But I know that I understand more now," said Johnny.

"I agree," said Tito. "I understand a lot more too." We went on driving through the narrow roads, passing lots of houses.

"Papi, are we going to the same village you were born in?" asked Johnny.

"That's right. But remember, I left with my mother and Tio for the States right after my father died when I was just a boy."

"How does it look to you now?" Tito asked.

"Different and yet a lot the same. I mean there are so many more people living in these here parts today. When I was a boy, you could see open country for miles. There wasn't a house in sight."

"I hope Tio will be happy here," said Mami.

"I think he will, Rosa. He has his two acres of land. Okay, there's no house yet, but he's going to build one. You should see how excited he is, talking to the contractors and the architect. Right now he's renting a small house next to my cousin Manuel."

We saw a sign saying BARRIO ANTULIO. Papi drove over a bridge. Underneath we saw a narrow river. The main part of town was just a paved road with several stores, a garage, a restaurant, and a few houses.

"We're going farther up," said Papi, "where Tio is, about less than a mile outside the village."

"Some village! There ain't even a movie or a plaza or nothing!" Tito looked disappointed.

We drove steadily uphill on a winding road and then Papi slowed down.

"Here we are, folks." He stopped the car in front of a small house that was painted pink with a blue trim. When we got out of the car, a rooster came over and stood across the road, looking at us.

"There's Tio Manuel's rooster, Yayo. Isn't he handsome?" said Papi. Yayo was handsome all right. He had a brilliant red comb and long shiny black feathers sprinkled with red tips and specks of dark green. It looked like he sparkled in the sunshine.

"Oh, Papi, he's so beautiful! Here, Yayo!" I called out to him. Yayo bobbed his head up and down, scratched his claws on the ground, and then came running toward me.

Quickly Papi jumped in front of Yayo, blocking him. "Don't—don't pet him, Felita! These roosters can be mean. He might snap at you." Papi lifted his arms and shooed Yayo away.

"Hello!" Tio rushed out, greeting us. "How wonderful to see all of you." He took us inside. "Isn't this a nice little house? It's small but it has everything we need. Rosa, Alberto, and Felita, you will be sleeping in this room. The boys will be sleeping next door with Manuel and Maria, since they got lots of room. Oh, yes, we are expected there for lunch, which is right now. So why don't we eat first and walk around later."

I was surprised to see Tio Jorge talking so much. He's not usually like that. For the first time all day I remembered that I was gonna stay here and live with him and not the rest of my family. It gave me this sinking feeling right down to my stomach.

Everything was happening so fast. Tio took us next door and introduced us to Tio Manuel and Tia

Maria. They had a big color T.V. in the living room. All the furniture had plastic covers. Shelves on the wall held religious pictures and statues. But there was one wall that was covered with old photographs. There were pictures of me and my brothers when we were real little and pictures of Papi when he was a boy. One very old picture showed a pretty girl smiling, and I knew it was my abuelita because she had her same smile even back then.

When we sat down to lunch, Tito was the first one to go for some food.

"Tito!" Tia Maria shook her finger at him. "This is a religious household. Here we don't eat unless we first thank the Lord for our food."

Tito got so embarrassed that he turned pink. We all lowered our heads as Tia Maria said grace. But Tio Manuel looked at me smiled and winked. I got the feeling he wasn't as religious as Tia Maria. After we had finished eating she took me aside. "You know, Felita," she said, "it's quiet around these here parts. The neighborhood hasn't any youngsters; there are mostly retired folks. But all the children, who are Catholic, of course, get together at our church. We have a youth center there with summer activities. After your parents and brothers leave, we'll take you over so that you can make friends.

"Also I want you to know that you will be treated here as if you were my very own child. You can come to me for anything that you need, anything at all. Understand?"

Oh, great, I thought, now I have to go to church to have fun. Boy, was I in an exciting place! But, no matter what I thought, I knew I had to be polite, so I said, "Thank you, Tia." After hearing that speech and putting together what I had already seen of Tia Maria, she is the last person I'd want to come to for anything, anything at all!

That evening as darkness was setting in, I lay on a cot next to my parents, trying to sleep. The noises were so loud that I kept jumping up. Here the coquís, the tiny green frogs that sing all over the Island, were almost drowned out by what sounded like a parrot talking in a weird language. Every couple of seconds it would stop and then begin laughing hysterically. Crickets were blasting away like they were having an argument and wanted to outshout each other. Bullfrogs were singing duets with what sounded like crows. At first I thought I'd never get to sleep, but soon I got used to the harsh noises and after a while it sounded like an orchestra was playing me a lullaby.

But the next day when I went to take my shower, I saw this huge brown bug flying right at me. I couldn't believe my eyes! It was a cockroach with wings. When it flapped its wings it sounded like whispers, *whifft . . . whiffttt*! Ugh! It was horrible! Then I looked up and thought I would faint. Over the shower a whole bunch of them were clinging to the ceiling. They looked absolutely disgusting. I ran out screaming with fear and told Mami there was no way I'd go into that shower.

"There's nothing to worry about." Mami tried to calm me down by telling me the bugs were completely harmless. "They don't bite or do you any harm. They only come out like that in the summer. We used to have them in the city when I was a girl, before Abuelo put screens and modern bathrooms in his house."

So now I'd have to live with these huge, ugly, disgusting flying cockroaches on top of everything else. I mean first there are no kids my own age around here to play with, then Tia Maria keeps talking about religion all the time . . . and of course Tio Jorge hardly talks at all.

At least back in San Juan there were a lot of people around and all kinds of places to visit and things to see. Here there wasn't anything I could look forward to. I was real tempted to ask Mami if I could go back home with them. But I felt too embarrassed to say I wanted to leave, so I took a deep breath, looked at Mami, and said, "Either they go or I go. I'm not staying here with those cockroaches. I mean it!"

"Don't worry, Felita, Tio Jorge will spray the bathroom today and Papi will seal up all the cracks so that they can't get in, okay?"

"I hope so."

"It will be all right. I promise you that Tio Jorge will spray every day from now on."

Late that afternoon things started looking up. Tio had invited some people over to meet us and among them were two girls around my own age.

"Felita, this is Provi and Gladys," said Tia Maria, introducing us. Me and the girls went out in back and sat down on the small patio.

"My mother says you're gonna be here all summer. Is that right?" Provi asked me.

"Right. I'm staying with my granduncle."

"Is this your first visit to Puerto Rico?" Gladys asked.

"Yes, we just finished visiting with my other relatives on my mother's side in San Juan."

"How do you like it so far?" asked Provi.

"I like it. We had such a great time . . . we went all over the Island and took in the sights."

"They told me you're from New York City," Gladys said. I nodded. "Well, this is even different from San Juan, or any other city. It's real quiet. But we like it."

"My grandmother was born here. She used to tell me all about this village and what it was like when she was a girl. Even though she lived in New York for many years, she always talked about her life here."

"Is she still alive?" Provi asked.

"No, she died two years ago. She's my Tio Jorge's sister. I mean she was."

"It would be nice if you would join our youth center over at Santa Teresa's, our church," said Provi. "It's Catholic. Are you Catholic?"

"Yes, I am. Tia Maria told me about it. I'm going with her this Friday."

"Oh, good!" Provi looked pleased. "You'll like it. We got lots of activities and play games and all. Besides, there's not much else to do here in the summer, so joining the center is a good idea."

"Felita! Felita!" I heard Tio Jorge calling me. "There are some guests who want to say good-bye to you." Finally, after I said good-bye to most of the people, I said good-bye to the girls.

"We'll see you Friday, Felita, at the church. It'll be nice."

At last I had something to look forward to.

That evening Mami made a long list of all the things she thought Tio Jorge and me would need.

"Rosa, we don't need half of these things." Tio was annoyed at her. "What are we supposed to do with more juice containers or dish towels? Or any of this junk? We got all we need and we'll be taking most of our meals over at Maria's. I don't see why you like to waste money!"

"Tio, please, don't argue. I know what I'm doing!" Mami was determined. "I'm not leaving you two here without the necessary things to make you comfortable." When Tio Jorge tried to argue back, Mami put up her hands. "It's settled." Tio walked away. When Mami got stubborn, he knew there was no way anyone else could win.

Even though I had brought some drawing materials with me from home, I put more stuff down on Mami's list. I asked for more oil crayons, colored pencils, and drawing pads, as well as a set of watercolors. To my surprise she agreed to get everything for me. Usually she fusses over what we spend. I was sure glad she was in a buying mood.

The next morning, after we had shopped in a large town called Rio Grande for the stuff on Mami's list, we all drove to Luquillo beach. It was beautiful there with rows of palm trees giving lots of shade. We went swimming in a bayside area where the water was shallow. The sand was almost white and the water such a clear green that you could see way down to your toes.

My brothers were going out of their way to be real nice to me. They carried me on their backs, let me win in tag, and made sure I always caught the ball. It was a wonderful afternoon and I kept on wishing it would never end. But soon Papi told us all it was time to leave. Tomorrow they had to get up early to catch the plane home.

Early the next day, as we were saying our goodbyes, Mami took Tia Maria and me aside.

"Felita, you mind Tia Maria, you hear? I want to hear nothing but good reports about you, understand?"

"Don't worry, Rosa," said Tia Maria. "I am a God-fearing woman and I'll take care of Felita like she was my own little girl. But if she does anything wrong, I'll make sure to let her know."

"My Felita is a good girl and I know she won't be a problem," said Mami. "But in case she is, please tell Tio Jorge and he'll let us know about it."

Even though I was annoyed at Mami for asking for good reports on me, I was also pleased that she'd said I was good. Mami reached over and hugged me. "I'm going to miss my baby so much. Don't forget to write, Felita. I want to hear from you at least once a week, you hear?"

Papi came over, lifted me up, and gave me a big hug and kiss.

"You are going to have a wonderful experience here, Felita. Now, I want you to listen to Tio Jorge and be a good girl, okay?"

"So long, Chinita . . ." Johnny hadn't called me that in ages. It used to be his nickname for me when I was little. "I'll miss not having to baby-sit for you."

"You show these people what us Puerto Ricans in the Big Apple are all about, Felita," Tito whispered to me, "and don't be coming back no hick. Educate them, you hear?" I had to laugh at Tito, and he made me feel less sad.

"Remember how much we all love you." Mami gave me a final hug.

"She'll do just fine here!" Tia Maria stood close to me as we watched them all drive off. "Now, Felita, this is not the city. You are in the country now and there isn't all the excitement you're used to. But there are other things you can do—read, sew, and of course go to church. And remember, you can come to me to talk, anytime."

"Thank you, Tia." I walked away fast, not wanting her to see how homesick I felt already.

My parents and brothers had been gone for almost a week. Every day since they'd left, Tio and I had followed the same boring routine. We got woken up at about five o'clock by the roosters just as the sun came up. They kept on crowing and making a terrible racket for at least a couple of more hours. At about seven Tio would check the shower for those flying roaches and spray before I went in to wash up.

I still hated those awful bugs. But there were a lot of other kinds besides—black spiders that were really dangerous and centipedes that bit. This was one place I knew I couldn't walk around in with bare feet, that was for sure. And, even though we had screens on all the windows and doors, the bugs always managed to get in somehow. We were always spraying or having to swat at them with our trusty flyswatters, which had turned out to be one of the more useful items on Mami's list.

Then we ate breakfast in our own cottage and got ready for the walk that Tio Jorge had planned the night before. He always promised to show me a lovely view or a farm where he was sure the owners would let me pet the animals and maybe even ride a horse. But so far we hadn't seen anything like he promised.

One morning after walking for a long time and not finding the place Tio Jorge was looking for, two mean guard dogs tried to attack us. It was a good thing they were behind a barbed wire fence, or else they would have attacked us. As if that wasn't bad enough, Tio started in with one of his speeches about how things have changed. "It's a disgrace the way people put up fences and have guard dogs! There's no place where people can walk freely anymore." And he went on like that nonstop.

I really liked my Tio Jorge much better the way he used to be back home when he hardly ever talked. He never gave me a hard time there, but now he was always grumbling and complaining like Tia Maria. He was definitely getting on my nerves.

To try and make things better after one of these

walks, Tio Jorge always took me to his property and told me where everything was going to be built—the house, the dog kennel, the vegetable garden, the chicken coop—everything! By the second day I already knew this by heart and was sick of hearing it again. But what really made me furious was Tio's stupid quiz game, where he asked me the name of flowers and birds in Spanish and English. When I was little this used to be fun, but not anymore. For example, he'd say, "Felita, tell me what is the name in Spanish of the spider plant?" I'd just act like I didn't hear him. You'd think he'd shut up, right? But he'd keep on going. "You know it's called mal padre. I'm surprised you forgot such an easy one."

After an hour or so of this, I'd just walk away and head down the road toward the cottage. No way was I gonna play his stupid game! When I got home, Tio was usually right behind me. By now he wasn't saying anything to me. I guess he took a hint to leave me alone.

By then it was time for the main meal of the day, which we all ate from about twelve thirty to one o'clock over at Tia Maria's. One thing I have to admit is that she was a real good cook and the food was always delicious. After eating, everyone took a nap. Once I got up I'd be all refreshed and ready to do something that was fun, but there was never anything to do. Tio Jorge didn't even have a T.V. He said he was going to buy one when he finished his house. At first I used to watch T.V. at Tia Maria's, but she was always watching her boring soap operas or reruns of old series like *Bonanza* or *Mission: Impossible*, where everyone was speaking Spanish.

The things I liked to do best in Barrio Antulio were to play out in the backyard with the animals and do my drawings. Today was no different. I went out to play with the guinea hens. They had bushy gray feathers speckled with white that went down around their feet. They looked like they were wearing woolen socks. One hen in particular was very talkative and kept following me around. I named her Lina, after my little cousin. There were also four rabbits. Three of them were all white and the fourth had black markings. I named him Vinny because he was different from the others. I also had learned how to handle Yayo the rooster. He could be mean all right. Every chance he got he'd sneak up on you and try to take a nip out of your leg. But with me he'd learned to take care, because whenever he came too close, I'd swat him with a branch.

Late in the afternoon I took out my sketching materials and sat out on the back patio. I'd been thinking a lot about my friends, especially Vinny. I missed him and Gigi the most of all. I felt like writing and telling them how lonely I was and how much I wanted to go home, but I knew I could never do such a thing. It would be too embarrassing. After all, everybody back home thought I was on this great vacation just having a wonderful time in P.R. How could I write and tell them that nothing was happening at all? I was happy at least I'd sent them the picture postcards so that they knew I had done some good things.

Right now they were probably all outside, playing like crazy and having fun. The more I thought about home, the worse I felt. Things had been going so good just before I left between me and Vinny, I just hoped and prayed he didn't find some other girl this summer that he liked more than me. Sooner or later I had to write to him and Gigi, but at this moment, I preferred later.

The one thing I had to look forward to was Friday when Tia Maria was taking me to the youth center at her church. I knew I would see Provi and Gladys again and get to meet some other kids and hang out. Then maybe I would have something good to write to my friends about.

I looked out at the wide view before me, ready to do some drawing. I had to admit that even if there wasn't much to do here, it sure was pretty. From where I sat I could see the surrounding mountains and all the houses, mules, horses, and square patches of earth where different vegetables were growing. Fruit trees stood next to tall palm trees that swayed in the breeze. The narrow country roads had cars and trucks going back and forth on them. There were a lot of things happening out there, but it was a quiet kind of busyness, not really noisy or disturbing like in the city.

I took a deep breath, inhaling the sweet and spicy smells of the flowers and vegetables all mixed up together. It felt really good to breathe this air. Then I picked up my pad and a large charcoal pencil. Maybe I'd start by drawing the sky. Today the cloud formations were so gigantic that I could make out animal forms and whole kingdoms in them. When the sun ducked behind the clouds, all the colors on the earth darkened and there were long shadows. When it reappeared, everything got bright again, dazzling my eyes. I began to sketch in all the outlines.

"It's just beautiful," I said aloud. And then I began putting the colors in my picture.

Today was Friday and Tia Maria was getting ready to take me to the youth center and church. She told me I also had to go to confession.

I absolutely refused. "I have my own priest at home, I'll go to confession when I get back," I told her. I mean church is all right, but confession is something I can live without.

Tia kept on insisting. "That's wrong, Felita. It's not proper that you be here almost two months without receiving the holy sacrament."

"Well, I'm not going."

"We'll see about that, young lady. I'm the one in charge of you."

"No, you're not! Tio Jorge is in charge of me. He's my real granduncle. Let's ask him."

"It's very rude of you to speak to me like that." Tia Maria clicked her tongue and shook her head. She had a habit of doing this every time she disapproved of anything. "I'll go to speak to Jorge right now!" she said and stormed over to Tio Jorge's. I waited a few minutes and then I went to see what was happening. Inside I could hear them arguing.

"I'm sure Rosa would certainly disapprove, Jorge. It's not proper for a girl her age to—"

"Listen, Maria, you are of course entitled to your opinion, and I appreciate that you're looking out for Felita. But she is my grandniece and I am the one who is responsible for her. If she doesn't want to go to confession, then she doesn't have to."

"Well, if that's the way you see it, Jorge, then there is little I can do to make sure Felita continues to live like a good Christian. I only hope you will answer to her mother for this and that I will not be blamed!"

"Yes, Maria, I will! I'll take full responsibility for this with both Rosa and Alberto. Satisfied? Now, I'm not gonna argue with you anymore, so that's that."

Boy, was I ever relieved to hear Tio's words! I kind of knew he'd back me up, since at home Tio never goes to church. He says that God is in nature and not in a building with ceremonies and statues.

I was real grateful to Tio, and felt sorry that lately I'd been so angry at him.

As we drove to the youth center Tia Maria sat next to Tio Manuel, sulking. I sat quietly looking out at the scenery. We passed lots of small churches along the way, like Pentecostal, Seventh Day Adventists, and different kinds of Baptists.

"Look"—Tio Manuel pointed to a small wooden cabin—"that looks like it's been converted to a church. Didn't that used to be a vegetable market?"

"Heaven help us all. It seems that nowadays anybody can convert a shack by putting up a sign and calling it a house of God." There Tia Maria went, clicking her tongue and shaking her head again.

"It's still better than having people hanging out in cafés and bars. Besides, Maria, they aren't harming anyone."

"Maybe so, Manuel, but I still say it's sacrilegious. But then who listens to me anyway? It seems all I'm good for is to cook and clean." I knew that remark was meant for me because of our argument about confession. I glanced over at Tio Manuel, who raised his eyes and kept silent.

When we got to Santa Teresa's, there were lots of cars there already. People were standing by the large old church, talking. I searched around until I spotted Provi and Gladys. I waved and they waved back. Tia introduced me to some of the parishioners and then to Father Gabriel, a short man with a friendly smile.

"This is Father Gabriel, our parish priest. My niece Felita, from the United States. She will be spending the summer with us."

"You are most welcome to our church, daughter," said Father Gabriel, smiling. I excused myself and went over to Provi and Gladys. They were now with a larger group of girls. Provi looked real happy to see me and introduced me to some of the other kids. "There's a large recreation room," she said, "and we have Ping-Pong and games. Come on, I'll show you around." We went into a very large airy room with high ceilings and enormous windows. There were two Ping-Pong tables, chairs, a couple of couches, and game tables. Two women dressed in brown suits and white blouses spoke to us. "Come in, young ladies. I see a new girl," the younger one said.

"This is Felita Maldonado, Sister Tomasina," said Provi. "She's visiting here for the summer from New York City."

"How nice," Sister Tomasina said.

"Do you understand us?" the older woman asked me. "Do you speak Spanish?"

"Yes, I do."

"Very good. This is Sister Tomasina and I am Sister Pilar. I'm glad you know Spanish. So many children who visit us from the United States don't know Spanish." She turned to the other kids. "Listen, listen, everyone here! This is Felita, a new girl. You

are all to make her feel comfortable and welcomed!"
Then Sister Pilar looked at me again. "What do you
like to do most, Felita?"

I wasn't prepared for that question, so I didn't
know what to answer. "Do you have something you
particularly like to do?" This time she spcke to me
like she was losing her patience.

"I like drawing best."

"All right. I think we have some crayons and pencils around here somewhere. Let me get them for
you."

"Oh, no," I said quickly. The last thing I wanted
to do today was draw. I did enough of that at Tio
Jorge's. "I'd just as soon do something else here. But
thank you, Sister."

"Very good"—Sister Pilar patted me on the arm—
"you'll find something to keep you busy, I'm sure."
I saw that there were mostly girls and only a very
few boys.

"Sister Pilar is really nice," Provi whispered to
me. "Don't let her way of talking put you off. Sometimes we call her 'the sergeant,' but she's buena
gente—really good people. Why don't we all go outside and bring a rope, in case we want to play?"

Gladys and four other girls, Anita, Marta, Judy,
and Saida, followed us out into a very large courtyard. Now I saw where most of the boys were. They
were busy playing basketball way over at the far end
of the yard.

"The boys around here are heavy into sports," Provi said. "That's Brother Osvaldo. He's the coach and he's also in charge of a lot of the summer activities." She pointed out a younger man wearing a gray jogging suit and blowing a whistle. "He's nice, we all like him."

We decided to jump rope. But since I didn't know the games in Spanish, Provi picked a simple one and explained it. "It's real easy, Felita. When it's your turn to jump, we'll all ask you, 'What are you going to be when you grow up? Single? Engaged? Widowed? Or married?' You have to answer, 'Married.' Only if you say married can you jump, since the next question we ask you is, 'How many kids will you have?' That's when you jump and we keep on counting with you, because the number of times you skip rope is as many kids as you're gonna have. You can keep on skipping until you miss or get too tired."

It was wonderful to be playing with kids my own age for a change. We were all good jumpers so most of the time we stopped because we got too tired to go on. One time I was going to have two hundred children! All of us laughed so hard we could hardly move. After a while we got bored with the game and sat under a large shady tree.

"What shall we do now?" asked Anita.

"Let's do rhymes," said Marta.

"Great idea"—Anita motioned to us—"let's form a circle and we'll go all around."

"But I don't know that game," I told them.

"It's easy, Felita. We'll teach you," said Anita. "You see, we all just repeat a rhyme and each girl tries to go faster than the last girl, until someone makes a mistake. Then she's out. We keep going until the last girl who says the rhyme fastest and correctly wins."

I was beginning to feel uneasy about my Spanish. "I don't know. I don't think I should play."

"Come on, Felita, at least try," said Marta.

"Say yes, so we can get on with the game," Anita said. "Come, let's go!"

I really didn't want to play this game, but I also didn't want to be left out, so I agreed.

"Okay, now listen to this rhyme," Anita said. "Pay attention, everybody.

> "Estaba la pájara pinta
> sentadita en su verde limón
> con el pico recoje la hoja,
> con la hoja recoje la flor.
> ay, mi amor, ay, mi amor."

It was a real tongue twister, about a little speckled bird who sat on a green lemon and with her beak picks up a leaf, and the leaf picks up a flower. It ended with "oh, my love, oh, my love." I didn't think I could handle it, but everyone was watching me, so I began repeating each sentence after Anita.

"Good, Felita," she said. "You go last. This way

you'll have more time to practice, right?" I really wanted to say forget it, since that meant I'd have to go faster than anyone else. But I also didn't want to chicken out. They started: Anita went, then Marta, Gladys, Saida, Judy, Provi, and finally it was my turn. I managed to get through the rhyme all right, but I was speaking so slowly, it was almost a joke. I could hear giggles coming from Anita and Marta. "Listen, Felita, you went too slow," said Anita, "but since this is your first time, you can stay in the game. But next time you better go faster."

They began again, going even faster than before, so fast that I could hardly understand the words anymore. When my turn came, I took a deep breath and tried to keep up, but the words came out even slower than before and I made some awful mistakes.

"You're out!" Anita yelled, then she and Marta laughed louder than anyone else. Provi smiled uncomfortably at me and I could see she was feeling bad too. They went right on with the game, going faster and faster until everyone missed except Anita. "I'm the winner!" she said. "Let's do another game." She said a rhyme that was even harder than the last one, and then she had the nerve to ask me to play again.

"Not me," I said. "I'm not playing."

"Come on, don't be so sensitive, Yankee!" When Anita said this, I couldn't believe my ears. I just stared at her. "Listen, gringita, all you have to do is try. Come on, now—"

"Hey!" I cut her right off. "My name is not Yankee or gringita, my name is Felita! Don't you call me by those names! You understand?" My Spanish became loud and clear.

"Stop being silly, everybody," said Provi. "Let's all do something else."

"Oh, sure," said Anita. "Let's do something different to please Ms. Nuyorican here from the big city, who is too good to play with us."

I walked right up to Anita, and I could feel everyone getting nervous. "I told you my name is Felita. And you better remember it if you're talking to me. Or are your ears stuck up your backside, stupid!" Anita backed off, looking surprised.

"Felita"—Provi stepped in between me and Anita —"she was only kidding around."

"Anita didn't mean anything bad," said Gladys. "You don't have to take it all so hard."

"Oh, yeah? I don't think it's funny to be called names. If you all came to New York and didn't know English so good, you'd make mistakes too, you know."

"That's true!" Anita said, smirking at me. "We'd make mistakes because we are Puerto Ricans. Since you are not Puerto Rican, what can we expect from you?"

Not Puerto Rican? Of course I am Puerto Rican. What was she talking about? "I am Puerto Rican." I could hear my own voice shaking.

"You can't be because you weren't born here. You're from over there." No one had ever said such a thing to me! I just stood there in front of Anita, speechless.

"Come on, that's enough of this. Let's go inside, Felita." Provi put her arm around my shoulder and took me inside. As soon as I walked in I bumped into Sister Pilar.

"Well, Felita, are you joining our church social club?" I nodded weakly at her. Actually I wasn't sure anymore about anything. "Good, very good. The age range is from nine to about fourteen so you will fit right in. We will be having some supper soon. Please help yourself." She walked off.

"Felita"—Provi held my hand—"don't you mind Anita and some of the others. They just like to tease and act smart when anyone from the States comes here. Especially if the person is from New York. It's sort of a game they play, that's all."

"Too bad, Provi, because I don't like playing that game; not at all. They can't tell me what I am. I know what I am."

"It was great the way you stood up to them, Felita, because a lot of the girls are scared to mess with them. Especially that Anita—she can be mean. Actually those two love giving everybody a hard time, even if you are from here. But listen, the others aren't bad, honest. Give them another chance, okay?"

"Okay." I started to feel a little better.

"Now let's eat." I followed Provi into another large room where tables were loaded with food, juice, and soft drinks. Everyone was helping themselves. The adults were seated in one area, talking. Little kids were running around, laughing and playing. Most of the boys sat apart from the girls. I realized that here the boys and girls seemed to mix much less than at home.

After we'd finished eating, and had helped clean up, Provi said, "How about coming over to my house tomorrow and eating with us?"

"Great!" I was happy that she asked me. "I have to get my aunt's permission first."

"Good, I'll go find my parents and tell them." When Provi returned with her parents, I was very surprised because they looked old enough to be her grandparents.

"It's okay for tomorrow, Felita. I'll come over early and pick you up."

On the way home Tia said, "I'm delighted that you and Provi like each other so much. Her parents, the Romeros, are friends of the family, so I know that they are decent religious people; definitely the type you should mingle with." I was glad to see that I had done one thing that made Tia Maria happy.

But later that night I just couldn't put what Anita

had said to me out of my mind. All my life I've been
Puerto Rican, now I'm told I'm not, that I'm a gringa.
Two years ago I got beaten up by a bunch of mean
girls when we had moved into an all-white neighborhood. I hadn't done anything to them, nothing. They
just hated me because I was Puerto Rican. My whole
family had fought back in that neighborhood until
we finally moved out. How could she say those things
to me? Even today, back home when anybody tries
to make us ashamed of being Puerto Rican, we all
stand up to them. What was Anita talking about?
It made no sense. At home I get called a "spick" and
here I'm a Nuyorican.

I wanted to go home! The tears started coming
and I couldn't hold them back. I was feeling pretty
miserable, helpless, and like I was trapped—exactly
like I felt two years ago. Back then, Abuelita had
told me to love myself instead of hating those girls;
that I should be proud of what I was, a Puerto Rican.
What advice would she give me now, here today,
when in her wonderful, precious Puerto Rico, I get
told I don't belong either? I wished I could write to
Mami and tell her I wanted to go home, that I hated
it here! But I knew I couldn't do that. Everyone would
be so disappointed in me; my folks who had saved
and sacrificed so I could be here, Tio Jorge, and even
Vinny, who had given me all those Spanish lessons.

After a while I stopped crying and took a deep
breath. I knew I was stuck here and that was all there

was to it. One thing was for sure, I wasn't telling Tío Jorge about what had happened. That was all he'd need to hear, right? Then he'd really say I should be hanging out with him, keeping him company instead of going over to the youth center, where they gave me a hard time.

Suddenly I remembered that tomorrow I was going over to Provi's. I really liked her. She reminded me of Gigi—understanding and kind. I yawned and closed my eyes. At least there was one person here I liked.

Provi's house was about a twenty-minute walk from Tio Jorge's. She had come to pick me up and we walked past the main road until we came to an area where there were a whole bunch of houses that looked almost exactly alike. When we got to her house, Mrs. Romero greeted me. "I hope you are good and hungry, Felita, because I made lots of food for you growing girls."

After we ate, we went to Provi's room for our siesta. She had a big double bed and we spread out. It felt almost like I was back home with Gigi on her bed and in her room. I told Provi all about Gigi.

"You miss her, don't you?"

"Sure, Gi's my best friend."

"Well, if you like, Felita, I'll be your best friend in Puerto Rico."

"I'd like that a lot. You know, Provi, I tell Gigi just about everything. So I'm gonna tell you about my boyfriend."

"You got a boyfriend?"

"Yes, at home. His name is Vinny and he's from Colombia in South America and he's real handsome." I told Provi about Vinny and how he first asked me about taking lessons together.

She loved that story. "Did he write to you yet?"

"No. But that's only because I haven't written to him. Now that you're my friend and we'll be going to the youth center together, I'll have some good news for him."

"Will you show me his letters?"

"Absolutely!"

"That would be great!" She gave me a little hug before we took our nap.

Provi and me began seeing each other every day now. She told me that she had a very large family—four older brothers and four older sisters. They were all married and lived or worked in another part of the Island, except for her sister Diana, who lived nearby. "She has a boy, Gino. He's my favorite nephew and so cute," said Provi. "I'm always baby-sitting for them. Maybe sometimes you can baby-sit with me.

You'll like them. Right now they are away in Maya-güez, visiting Raymond's parents. He's her husband. We'll go there as soon as they get back, okay?" Provi told me that everyone in her family was way older than her. "I have nieces and nephews who are even older than me. Mami says that because I came to her late in life, I'm almost like an only child." I loved being with Provi. We would take walks, listen to music, and just hang out mostly in her house. But since I began spending so much time with Provi, Tio Jorge started grumbling and complaining.

"Going out again? I suppose that means you're not coming for our walk today."

Mostly I ignored him, but after a while I told him how I felt about Provi. "Tio, she happens to be my best friend here, and practically my only friend."

On Friday, Provi and I went to Santa Teresa's together, but I was still worried that Anita and Marta might start up with me again. Provi, Saida, Judy, Gladys, and me went to play outside. We jumped rope for a while and then hung out. Some of the boys came by and asked if we wanted to play with them. "Basketball practice is canceled. You wanna start a game or something?" Two boys named Ismael and Danny asked us. We agreed. "Good, let me get some more kids," Ismael said. When he returned, he brought Anita, Marta, and a couple of other girls.

"Now's a good time to all be friends," said Provi.

"I didn't start it"—I shrugged—"but I'm willing

if they are." I caught Marta's eye and smiled. She nodded quickly and turned away. Anita ignored me, so I ignored her too. While everyone was figuring out what to play, I came up with an idea. "Hey, everybody, I know this great game we play back home. It's called Simon says, it's so much fun. We pick a leader, who tells everybody what to do, and then you have to follow the exact instructions—"

"Big deal!" Anita cut me off. "That's just like playing follow-the-leader. What's the big—"

"No, it ain't," I said interrupting her right back, "because the leader has to say 'Simon says do this.' If they only say 'Do this' and you follow orders, you're out. It's very tricky."

"It sounds like a stupid game!" said Anita.

"Why?" I asked her. "Are you afraid to play it?" Some of the kids began giggling and I could see she was annoyed, so I didn't let up. "Maybe you're scared you can't keep up with a New York City game."

"I'm not the least bit scared to play," she said. "It's just that I think it sounds like a silly game."

"Well, you won't know till you try it, right?" I looked at the other kids. "Anybody else here afraid to play this game? I know one thing, back home we don't back out."

"I'll play," said Saida.

"Me too." Judy stood next to me.

"Hey, why not!" Ismael agreed. And then everybody else said they were in the game too.

"Well?" I looked at Anita and Marta. "You still chicken?" Anita looked real angry, but she said that she'd play. Naturally Marta did what Anita wanted, just like she was Anita's little slave.

"Since you're the one that knows the game," Provi said, "why don't you be the leader the first time." That was just what I wanted to hear! Today, Anita was getting hers, and right in front of everybody too.

I started out real simple, saying, "Simon says" put your hands on your head, touch your toes, scratch your ears, cross your eyes, stuff like that. But after a while I began going real fast, and when I didn't say "Simon says," some of the kids didn't catch it and they were out. Soon there were only five of us left in the game: Ismael, Danny, Saida, Marta, and Anita.

"What's the big deal about this great New York City game?" said Anita scornfully. "So far it reminds me of the games I played in kindergarten."

Great, I thought, Big Mouth is walking right into my plans.

"All right, Anita," I said. "Since you think this is too easy, I'll make it a little harder." I stepped back and gave myself some space. "Simon says do exactly what I do!" I went forward and did a cartwheel, something I was pretty good at. I could see that everyone was surprised. Ismael, Danny, Saida, and Anita did cartwheels too, but Marta couldn't make it and she fell. Then I did two quick cartwheels and waited. This time Saida couldn't make it and she dropped out. All the kids were watching to see who could hold out the longest. I wasn't even really playing Simon says anymore, I was just gonna make sure Anita got what she gave me and then some.

"Hey, Anita, like I know this is still real easy for you . . . kindergarten stuff, right? Now, let's see if you can do a little better!"

Anita gave me a real sarcastic smile. "Just keep on going and don't you worry about me!" she said.

Wonderful, I thought, and stepped back, giving myself a whole lot of room, then I shouted, "Simon says do this!" I bent backward making an arch with my back and touching my heels, then I leapt forward and did three quick cartwheels! I could see that all the kids were impressed. I stopped smiling and waited, staring at Anita. Ismael went first and missed. Then Danny went. He was a little slow, but he got through. Now everyone was looking at Anita. She was real nervous and cleared a large space for herself. When she bent backward, she hardly touched her heels and then she managed one cartwheel and on the second one she tripped and fell. Everyone started laughing because she looked so funny scrambling all over the grass, trying to get up.

"Too bad, Anita, but you're out!" I yelled. "Danny is the leader now! Maybe you should go back to kindergarten, Anita." I was laughing louder than anyone.

"I think this is a game for morons!" Anita shouted back at me. She was still dusting herself off from the fall. Marta and Gladys were busy trying to help her. "I'd rather play a game of tag than this stupid game!"

"Why? What's the matter, Anita? New York City games are too hard for you?" I was feeling good now because I had really shown her up. Anita walked away, followed by Marta, Gladys, and Ismael. Just as Danny was trying to set up another game of Simon says, I heard Anita shouting real loud in jeringonza, which is like Spanish pig latin. I couldn't make it out exactly, but I knew how it went, because Provi was teaching me. I could make out, "Felita gringita go home," and some kids were laughing and looking at me. I got so furious at Anita that I walked right over to her. "Listen, Anita, you got something to say to me?" I made sure everyone heard me too. "Say it to my face!"

Anita sure wasn't expecting me to confront her. "I wasn't talking to you," she said and tried to walk away, but I stepped right in front of her.

"No, not to me. About me! I understand when you say my name and also the nasty thing you were saying about me." All the kids started to gather around us. Anita stood perfectly still. "Well?" I said. I wasn't gonna let her walk away, we were gonna settle this here and now!

"All right, then!" She looked around at the crowd

of kids. "You don't belong here. Why don't you go back to your Yankee country!"

"Don't you tell me what to do, you stupid hick! I can be here all I want, you don't own this place!"

"Show-off! Braggart!" she yelled back.

"Moron! You have as much brains as a brick!" I screamed. When Anita leaned toward me, I clenched my fists and took a stance, ready to punch her one. "Come on, I dare you. Come on! Try something, do me a favor! Just call me one more name and you'll eat it for lunch!" Boy, I really wanted to wallop her one right on her smug face!

"Oh-oh," said a boy named Julian, "the girls are gonna have a fight!"

"Cut it out," said Provi. She and Saida tried to step in between us, but I blocked them, moving closer to Anita. Anita stepped back and I went toward her, waiting.

"One more word, Anita." She must have really heard my warning because she shrugged and slowly began to back off.

"Come on," said Saida. "Let's quit this and all be friends."

Anita turned away and stood right in the middle of the crowd of kids. Then she pointed to me. "I'm not being friends with that one! Anybody who's her friend can forget about being friends with me!" With that she turned and walked away. Marta went with her and I was sad to see Gladys go too.

"Why does she keep calling me names?" I asked as I walked away with Provi, Saida, and Judy.

"Anita's always been a troublemaker," said Saida. "Remember when she got on Maria's case?"

"That's right," Judy said. "Maria was a girl who was here last summer and she had a lisp when she talked. Right away, Anita starts talking behind her back and making fun of her. She's just nasty, and so is her sidekick Marta."

"You were great standing up to her," said Provi.

"Really, Felita, it was good to see." Saida laughed.

"Absolutely," said Judy. "I loved Anita's face when she had to back off."

As we walked into the game room everyone became quiet and looked up at me. I guess the word had gotten around about my run-in with Anita. I saw Anita and Marta sitting with some of the kids on one of the couches. We went and sat at the other end of the room.

"Tell us something about where you live, Felita," said Judy. I told them about my friends, my block, and my school.

"It sounds like you and your friends do such exciting things," said Saida. "Tell us about some of the things you all do there."

"All right, let's see. Did you ever hear about a place called Chinatown?"

"We got a Chinese take-out food place up on

Highway Number Three, near Rio Grande," Judy said.

"Felita's talking about a whole town, right?" said Provi.

"Almost. It's actually a big section right in New York City that's called Chinatown. Lots and lots of Chinese people live there. They got shops selling clothes, toys—all kinds of Chinese things. Of course, the food tastes fantastic! They even have Chinese movies there."

"Did you ever see one?" asked Judy.

"No, I wouldn't understand one word if I did. Also, we have the Museum of Natural History, and there's a skeleton of a real dinosaur that's bigger than this whole church. It's enormous! And they have mummies and all kinds of nature displays. I love going there."

"Now," Provi said, "please tell us about snow, Felita."

"Oh, yeah, tell us," said Saida. "I would love to see snow."

"Okay. When the snow first falls, it's just great. It looks like magic when it comes from the sky. The snow can get so deep that you can hardly walk. You sink right to your knees, and traffic can't even move. Everything gets very still and quiet. But the best part is that school is shut down. The grown-ups hate it, but we love it because we can build forts and tunnels and we have snowball fights!"

"Did you ever taste snow?" asked Provi. "What does it taste like?"

"It tastes just like frozen ices but without any flavor." They kept on asking questions and I went on talking. I was enjoying telling about home and seeing how they were all impressed. From the corner of my eye I saw Anita, Marta, and her group leave the game room.

Provi and me were becoming better friends, and getting real tight. One day she took me to visit her sister Diana. We walked up a back road until we reached a big house built on two levels with terraces all around. A boy about four years old ran toward us. "Provi, Provi," he called out.

A woman who was very pregnant followed him. "You have to be Felita," she said. "I've heard so much about you from Provi. I'm Diana and that's Gino." She touched Gino's head gently. The house was real spacious. Inside there were lots of colorful framed posters and artwork on the walls. And so many bookcases filled with books! I had never seen so many books except for in the library. Diana gave us fresh pineapple juice with lots of crushed ice and we sat out on the top terrace. I told Diana all about my family, my neighborhood, school, and even about Abuelita and Tio. It was very easy to talk to her because she listened and was real interested. Gino was sitting on Provi's lap and kept on hugging her.

"Gino"—Diana tugged at his arm—"you are going to strangle your Aunt Provi. Felita, you have to understand that those two have a love affair going on, but that's also because she spoils him."

"I'm gonna marry Provi when I grow up," Gino said. "We already made plans." Provi winked at me.

"Where are you gonna live when you get married?" I teased him.

"Right here, in my room. I'm gonna get a bigger bed." That Gino was such a character.

"When are you having your baby?" I asked Diana.

"In about six weeks."

"If it's a girl, she'll name it after me, Providencia, right?"

"We'll see." Diana smiled. "I thought Maria-Elena would be a good name."

"Get out." Provi made a face. "That's so ordinary. Providencia is more unusual."

"Will you still love me the best if it's a girl?" Gino asked Provi.

"I'll always love you the best, silly." Provi hugged him.

That afternoon we had so much fun. I especially loved their library. They had all kinds of books in English and Spanish. When Diana paid me a compliment on my Spanish, I told her about what happened at the youth center.

"What? That's terrible!" Diana said. "But it does happen a lot here. Listen, when Raymond first got here after living in Philadelphia for about thirteen years, they teased him too. They do it, I think, because they feel that the Puerto Ricans who leave and then come back want to be accepted without having made any contributions to Puerto Rico. What they forget is that the reason most Puerto Ricans had to leave in the first place was on account of poor conditions here at home. Felita, it's wrong, but then, people aren't always smart or fair either."

I'd been looking at two art books and before we left, Diana told me I could borrow them. "Don't rush, keep them awhile and enjoy yourself before you return them."

That evening I looked at the books again. One had pictures showing the work of an artist named Francisco Goya, who lived in Spain a very long time ago. He painted kings, queens, palaces, war scenes, and even the countryside. I was amazed at all the different things he could paint. The other book showed the work of a Mexican artist, Diego Rivera. It had pictures of the Indians and the Spanish conquistadors and the Mexican revolution. It was like each picture was telling a story. I decided one way I could improve my drawings would be by studying the books. Someday I wanted to draw as good as these artists. Before I left this Island, I decided I was gonna do some good drawings, that was for sure.

It had been nearly a week since I'd spent time with Tio. But the morning after my visit to Diana he started in on me.

"Felita, when are you coming out to see the property with me? They are going to start digging the well soon."

"I don't know, Tio." I really wasn't in the mood to go out there and listen to his lectures, take a quiz, and then watch a bunch of men working. It was too boring.

"I thought we might walk over this morning, and you could see all the work that's being done."

"Tio, I'm supposed to see Provi, so I can't."

"Are you planning to have lunch there too?" He looked real annoyed.

"They did invite me, Tio, and I did say yes."

"Well, now I'm inviting you to spend some time with your own family. Even Tia Maria is complaining that you hardly eat here anymore."

"Tia Maria is always complaining about something!" I really wished he'd stop. "Look, Tio, I'll have lunch with everybody here tomorrow, I promise."

"Will you come out to the property too?"

"Do I have to?"

"No, you don't have to." Now I could see that he was hurt. "I just thought you might like to, that you would be interested. After all, I'm not just doing this for me. I want what I'm doing to be for all of us."

"Tio, I have so many other things to do."

"Suit yourself, Felita," he said.

"All right, Tio." I felt sorry to see him looking like that, so sad and all. "I'll go tomorrow with you."

"Very good, Felita, and you will see all the changes that have taken place on the property. Also, this way you can continue to learn about nature. I'll bet you have already forgotten all the things I taught you."

"No, I haven't."

"You want to prove it to me? Tell me now, what is the name of the white flower that is about four inches in circumference that blooms only at night and has a sweet fragrance?" I couldn't believe my own ears. Here he was quizzing me and I hadn't even finished eating breakfast. It was just too much!

There was no way I was gonna answer any of his dopey questions. "I don't remember, Tio," I said.

"See? I told you. I knew you would forget. But try to remember, come on. I'll give you a hint. It has a sweet fragrance much like—"

"I can't guess!" I cut him right off.

"What? I don't believe it. You're just not trying, come on."

"Stop it!" I yelled. "I don't wanna guess, all right? Can't you stop treating me like I'm six years old? Can't you have a normal conversation like a person, instead of acting like I'm a quiz kid? You make me sick and tired with all your stupid lectures and dumb questions. Leave me alone, you hear? Leave me alone!" I was so angry at Tio I felt myself shaking.

I got up and ran out to the patio because at that moment I couldn't stand being in the same room with him, I just couldn't! I stayed out back until I heard Tio Jorge leaving to go to his property. I felt relieved that he was gone and I almost wished he would stay away forever. Who needed him and all his boring information anyway? I decided to hang out and read until it was time to meet Provi.

The next day at breakfast Tio and me ate and hardly said one word. I knew I had been disrespectful toward Tio, and if my parents knew, I'd probably get the punishment of my life. After all, I was supposed to be spending the summer with him—that's why my parents had sent me here in the first place.

I looked over at Tio Jorge as he ate his breakfast, and kept hoping he'd ask me out to see his property today, but he never said a word to me. I guess he was waiting for me to apologize, and I knew I should, since I was the one who blew up and lost my temper. Still, I couldn't. When he left without me, I didn't say anything. I figured that sooner or later I'd make it up to him somehow. Besides, today I was having lunch with him at Tia Maria's. As far as I was concerned, that was a big enough sacrifice.

When I got over to Tia Maria's for lunch, she opened up her mouth against me. "My, look who's here. Felita, I see you are gracing us with your presence today. I was beginning to wonder if Provi's family shouldn't get paid for your meals instead of me from now on." She shook her head and clicked her tongue at least three times in my direction. I turned away and decided to ignore her. I didn't want to start any more trouble. But as soon as we sat down and started eating, she began complaining again—not about me, but about everything!

"Did you see what they are doing over by the old Rivera property? Putting up more houses. They don't stop coming up here—all that riffraff from the city. They are the ones responsible for so many bars and cafés opening up, I'm sure of it. Bad people bring bad habits."

"You're right," said Tio Jorge. "They are killing the countryside. Pretty soon there isn't going to be any countryside left." If the two of them didn't stop this conversation, I knew I was going to lose my appetite. I was sick of hearing each and every time about how wonderful the olden days were.

"We always had a finer quality of people then, not like today," said Tia Maria, clicking her tongue. It was just once too much! All I could do was push my plate away and ask to be excused. Everyone stopped eating and stared at me. "You haven't touched a thing, Felita. What's the matter with you?" asked Tia Maria.

"I'm not hungry."

"What's wrong with you—are you sick?" She just wouldn't let up on me.

"Yes, and I'd like to be excused. May I go, please?"

"Not until you tell us what's wrong with you!" Tia's voice sounded real impatient. "First you never eat here and now you aren't hungry. I'd like to hear an explanation." I was feeling so rotten, I felt like running out of there. "I'm waiting for an answer, young lady. Don't think you are—"

"Go on, Felita." Tio Jorge cut her off. "Go next door and lie down. I'll be in to see you in a few minutes." As soon as Tio Jorge said that, I bolted. I could hear him and Tia Maria arguing. I went straight to my room and sat down on my bed. I hated it here so much. If I had to stay in P.R., I wished I could live with Provi and Diana instead of with a bunch of complaining old people!

"Felita!" I heard Tio come into my room. "Felita, something is wrong and you must tell me what it is." He sat down next to me. "I don't want you to be unhappy. That was not the purpose of your visit here." He reached over and stroked my hair. "Do you miss home?" That was all he had to ask me. Suddenly I felt this heavy feeling coming over me. It was a sadness that went right to my chest and then to my throat. When I opened up my mouth to speak, I began to cry instead. Tio leaned over and held me, and right then I let loose a fountain of tears. "That's all right, Felita, go on, it's good to cry. That's right, let yourself go and cry all you want." After a while I couldn't cry anymore, and the tears stopped. Tio gave me a tissue and I blew my nose and wiped my face. "Feeling better?" he asked.

I nodded. "Tio, I'm sorry I yelled at you yesterday. I didn't mean what I said about you making me sick, honest."

"I know that." Tio squeezed my hand.

"It's just that I get tired of you saying the same old things to me over and over again, and I'd like to do something else besides looking at and talking about flowers and birds. And I'm sick of Tia Maria and Tio Manuel and all of you telling me how wonderful things used to be in the good old days. I wasn't here in the 'old days' and I don't care, okay? I like it now, right now! In this world today where I was born it suits me just fine. I don't wanna hear about what I'm missing for not being around when you were a kid. I'm a kid today and I'm content with the world, so just quit it! Okay?"

"Okay. Now I see, Felita. I just didn't understand that it must be hard for you to be here with three old people like us. You must be bored a lot, right?" I just looked at Tio and said nothing. "Listen, Felita, I'm going to ask you something that's very important and I want you to answer me truthfully. Promise?"

"I promise."

"Do you want to go back home?" I sure wasn't expecting him to ask me that question. I didn't know what to say. "If you do, it's all right. I understand,

and I will write to Rosa and Alberto and explain. They will understand too, so you needn't worry."

"I don't know, Tio. Honest." It was the truth. Part of me wanted to leave, but there was another part that wanted to stay.

"Well, I want you to think about it and let me know. I'll be honest too, Felita. I want you to stay with me very much, but only if you are happy. And I now see that you should spend as much time with your friend Provi as you like. This is your vacation and you are supposed to be having a good time. Maybe we could start over and not expect so much from each other. Neither one of us can take the place of the family or expect things to be like they were back home—and in my case like they were when I was a young man here. We'll both accept things as they really are. What do you say; will you think it over?"

"All right, Tio."

"Good, Felita. And remember you can always go back home, no one will force you to stay here." Tio got up to leave.

"Tio, one more thing. Please don't tell Tia Maria."

"Not a word, this is strictly between us." Tio put a finger over his mouth. "Now, I'm gonna finish my meal. If you like, I'll bring some food back for you."

"Thanks, Tio, I'd like that." I took a deep breath and lay down, feeling tired and relieved.

Life with Tio Jorge had become more relaxed now that we understood each other. He stopped pressuring me about having to hang out with him and didn't complain about my seeing too much of Provi. Also, I had gotten real used to things around here. Like just a couple of days ago, Tio Jorge pointed out to me that I had stopped screaming at the flying roaches. Instead I ignored them or swatted them out of my way. I'd also begun to sweep the spiders and centipedes out of the back door with a broom when I saw them.

"You are becoming a jíbara, a real country girl." Tio looked real pleased. "Your abuelita would be proud of you if she could see you. I know I am."

In fact things were going so good that this evening after I wrote my usual weekly letter to my parents, I decided to finally write Gigi and Vinny.

I wrote Gigi about the youth center and the nice kids there and all about Provi. I saved Vinny's letter for last. Lately I had been thinking about him a lot and wishing I could see him. I hadn't met one boy at the center that I liked even a little teeny bit, compared to how much I liked Vinny. I couldn't help worrying and wondering if he still liked me. Maybe he had found some girl he liked better than me. Just the thought of such a thing upset me. I wrote him a very long letter with my return address nice and clear. I told him too about all the good things that were happening. I wrote that I was still his girlfriend and still wanted him to be my boyfriend. Then I signed the letter with a heart and I drew little palm trees and kisses. Before I sealed it, I prayed that he would like it and write back soon.

In none of the letters did I ever mention Anita, Marta, and their little clique. I didn't want to write about those girls or think about them. In fact I wanted to make believe they didn't even exist.

Friday at Santa Teresa's,
Father Gabriel announced that we were putting on a
big carnival to raise money for the church. There
was one theme, he said, that was going to guide the
event. Its theme was to be the history of the Tainos,
who were the original inhabitants of Puerto Rico. We
were going to run a raffle and set up stands with
food, arts and crafts, books, and other things for
sale. But the best part was that the youth center was
going to put on a historical play and charge admis-
sion. The play was gonna have costumes, sets, and
music. It was scheduled for August 16th.

"All right, now," Father told us, "Sister Tomasina,

Sister Pilar, and Brother Osvaldo will take charge of the youth center. You kids work with them." They took us aside and Sister Pilar spoke to us.

"When the Spaniards came here looking for gold, contrary to what some historians have said, the Taino Indians who lived here did not give in easily; they fought back bravely. Now, I'm sure most of you know all this. However, I'm reminding you again to get you into the spirit of things. Sister Tomasina has written a script with the help of Don Antonio Diaz-Royo, who is one of our musicians." As Sister spoke I realized that I didn't know anything about the Tainos. Nobody back home had taught me this history.

When they began to call for volunteers, kids who wanted to audition or help in different ways, I raised my hand to work on the sets. I explained about the experience I had at school back home.

"She's great!" said Provi. "I've seen her drawings, Sister."

"So is Danny!" Ismael called out. "He's the best artist here."

"Danny, what do you say?" Brother Osvaldo asked. "Do you want to work on the sets?"

"Sure." Danny stood up.

"Good," Brother said. "You and Felita can work together."

We spent most of that afternoon and evening making plans. The two sisters and Brother Osvaldo were busying figuring out just who was going to do what. Before we left, everyone was assigned a job and given a copy of the script.

On my way to the car I had to pass Anita and Marta. I wasn't gonna look in their direction, since I sure didn't want to start nothing. But right when I was walking by them, I heard Anita's fat mouth.

"It sure is boring without any snow falling here like magic from the sky. Don't you think so? I hope it snows soon so we can all play at making little snowmen and having little snowball fights. Just like little babies!" Right away Marta and Gladys began laughing real loud to make sure I heard. I wanted to turn around and ask Anita if she would like a little smack up side her head. But instead I kept on walking and acted like I didn't hear a word.

When I told Provi what happened, she said I did the right thing to ignore them, because all they wanted was to make trouble. Even though I was annoyed, I was too excited about the scenery I was going to work on to really worry about Anita and Marta. I was gonna make the best sets possible and show them all around here what a person from New York City could do.

As soon as I got home I read the script. I learned that the Tainos were great fishermen and farmers. But when the Spaniards came, they used them for slaves and killed them for their gold. Some of the important leaders were women chiefs called caciques;

they were very famous and strong. I liked that.

On Sunday afternoon when I was at Diana's, her husband Raymond gave me a book with illustrations on Taino history. "Read this, Felita," he said, "and you'll learn even more about the Tainos." Raymond was so nice. In fact his soft way of speaking reminded me of my brother Johnny.

From now until the carnival we were supposed to be at Santa Teresa's early every Monday, Wednesday, and Friday for work and rehearsals.

"Some of you might have to be here even more often," said Brother Osvaldo, "so you better know that before you take on a job. I don't want any excuses later."

That sure didn't bother me any. In fact I was glad because it meant I didn't have to worry about spending time with Tio and his boring property, or being with Tia Maria and hearing all her complaining. I could at least be having fun with kids my own age, working on sets, and painting and drawing, which I love to do. As far as I was concerned, I'd be happy to spend the rest of my vacation at Santa Teresa's.

On Monday, Provi's father dropped us off and we got to work right away. The stage was being set up in the courtyard area where the boys played basketball. Brother Osvaldo and another man, a carpenter who everyone called Jackie, were finishing the platform for the stage as well as a large wooden backdrop that folded into several panels. So far Danny and me were the only artists. The sisters were trying to get us some helpers.

"Now," Brother told us, "you two have to study what a Taino village looked like and paint it to look as real as possible on this backdrop. I suggest you two get together and do some sketches. Use this book." He gave us the same book that Raymond had given me. "I've marked out some illustrations, see? These are good examples of scenes to work on. Now let's see what you two can do."

Danny and me struggled, trying to work from the book, and we kept getting in each other's way.

"Look, I have the same book at home," I said. "Why don't you take this one to your house and work on the sketches there. Meanwhile I'll work on my sketches too. Next time we can compare our work and figure out who should do what on the scenery."

"That's a great idea," said Danny. "What are you better at, people or landscapes?"

"I like to do everything. How about you, Danny?"

"Me too."

"All right, then let's each do one whole scene and see who does what things best."

At home as I worked on my scene, I could see the improvement in my drawing ever since I'd been copying the pictures in the art books Diana had lent me.

On Wednesday when we came in with our

sketches, Brother was real pleased. "Felita, this is beautiful work, you can really draw."

"I think you are better with people and animals than me," said Danny. "In fact you are better at mostly everything you did."

Brother Osvaldo decided that I would do all the figures and fine detail and Danny would concentrate on the buildings and background areas. We were also helping to make large cardboard cutouts of rocks, trees, and plants. Brother got us two helpers, Saida and Ismael. They were good at art, but not as good as me and Danny. Right away Ismael started getting bossy with me and Saida, ordering us around, saying things like, "Pick that up, Saida, and bring it here." Or to me, "Why don't you work on this side instead of where you are?" I mostly ignored him and told Saida to do the same. But when he started trying to change the way he was supposed to paint, I had to stop him.

"Ismael, I told you to make that background this here color." I pointed to the color I had mixed for him.

"No, Felita, I think it's better a dark brown."

"No, it's not! You won't be able to see that color from far off."

Ismael refused to listen to me, so I had to get Danny, who was working at the other end of the stage. Danny and Ismael are both about twelve, but I could see that Danny was tougher. "All right,

Ismael, Felita and me are in charge here. Just do it like she says." Danny stood facing Ismael with his hands folded. "I'm waiting, so don't be giving us a hard time."

Ismael smiled then bowed to me. "Anything you say, Miss Nuyorican!"

"My name is Felita!" I wasn't going to let that fool start in on me. "Don't you call me anything else except my name, you understand?" Ismael just grinned at me and went to work without saying a word. I looked at Saida and Danny, furious and fed up with being called names. Saida stuck her tongue out at Ismael. Danny walked back to where he was working. I just threw up my hands. There was too much to do to keep fighting.

Everyone was working like mad at Santa Teresa's, trying to get everything finished by August 16th. It was really looking good too. Colorful booths, tables, and posts were being completed. The stage sets looked better each time we worked on them. Some of the kids came by just to look at the way we did them. "Nice job, Felita. You guys are doing a great job." When they said those things, it made me feel good. I was really beginning to feel like I fit in at Santa Teresa's just like anybody else.

Anita and Marta had parts as Taino women. Anita had to say about two words and Marta didn't have any lines. Gladys was working on the costumes. She usually acted like I wasn't even around, but Anita and Marta were nasty. They would pass by where I was working, point to some of the sets I had done, and burst out laughing. I just kept on ignoring them like they were two morons. But one day it got to be just too much. I saw all three of them coming close to the sets, then I heard Anita's fat mouth.

"What is that?" She pointed to what I was working on. "I don't see no tall buildings, no Chinatown, and no snow, do you? How boring! What are we all gonna do?" She said this real loud, so everybody could hear.

Then her stooge Marta answered, "I guess we better go back to the big city, where everything is so exciting!" They all began to laugh, Gladys louder than anybody else. Right then I took a large brush I was holding, dipped it into a can of green paint, and got ready to paint their faces. But Saida stepped in front of me.

"Don't start nothing, Felita. Can't you see that's what they want? To make trouble so that we can't go on working and you can't finish the sets?" Mad as I was, I knew she was right. So I stopped, turned right around, and went back to work. I heard all three of them laughing as they walked away. I felt like yelling back at them, but I didn't. I glanced over at Danny and Ismael, and they were working too, just as if nothing had happened.

When I told Provi, she said she was surprised at Gladys. "She used to be my good friend right up to this year."

"I'm sorry," I said. "I know you like her."

"Not anymore. She can hang out with them if she likes," said Provi. "It's her loss."

Things were quiet for several days. Then late one evening, when I was finishing my work, I realized I needed more rags to clean my brushes and wipe up. So I headed toward the church to find Sister Tomasina. Around the back I bumped into Anita, Marta, and Gladys. They looked very startled, and turned away from me, acting real nervous. Then as I went inside I heard them giggling. There was something weird about their being together like that so secretively. It gave me the creeps. I found Sister, who gave me some rags, and rushed back, thinking maybe I could do a little more work before I left. But I looked inside the paint cans and couldn't believe it! There was no paint left. I looked inside every single can, six cans in all, and each one was empty. I looked around. Saida was nowhere in sight, Danny was working with Ismael on a large cardboard cutout, and the kids who had been rehearsing near the main building were gone. I just stood there not believing what I'd seen. Finally I ran over to the boys. "Danny, Ismael, the paint's gone! Come quick. There's no more paint in the cans. Look!"

They both followed me back. "Hey, look!" said Danny. "You're right. What happened?"

"That's what I'd like to know. Did you two see anything?" I asked. They both shook their heads, and when Saida came back, she also said she'd seen nothing.

"We'd better go inside and tell the sisters what's happened," said Danny.

"I bet I know what happened," I said. "I just saw Anita, Marta, and Gladys out back and they were acting real strange."

"Do you think they took the paint, Felita?" asked Saida.

"Definitely."

"Wait a minute." Ismael cut me off. "How do you know it was them that took it? Did you see them? Did anybody here see them? No, right?" It was true none of us had seen them nearby. Still, I was sure it had been them.

"Maybe we didn't see them," I said, "but they've been bugging me and trying to make trouble. I don't know anybody else who would do this. I just think they're out to mess things up."

"Just because you're fighting with them and can't get along with people here, don't mean that they did it," said Ismael. "You better be careful what you say, Felita. You can't be accusing people unless you got some proof. After all, they've been coming to the youth center a lot longer than you."

"I'm not the one that started it and I'm not the one fighting with them. You've all seen how they're always coming around trying to bother me and calling me names."

"You just better have proof, Felita, that's all I'm saying. I was here and I didn't see Anita, Marta, or Gladys anywhere around. And neither did anybody else." When I saw the smirk on Ismael's face, I didn't trust him either. But I also didn't feel so sure anymore about accusing Anita and Marta without proof. I didn't like it; in fact I was pretty angry, but I kept quiet and we all followed Ismael inside to tell the adults what had happened.

A few minutes later Father Gabriel, Sister Pilar, Sister Tomasina, Brother Osvaldo, and the rest of us searched all over the place to see if the paint had been spilled somewhere. But we didn't find any paint, not a single drop! I kept explaining that I hadn't used up the paints and Saida and Danny backed me up.

"This is terrible, just terrible!" said Sister Pilar. "We are so short of money. Those cans were a donation from the Fernandez hardware store. Now we have to get more." She looked at me and Danny. "How much more work do we have left?"

"We're a little less than halfway done," I said.

"And it's looking so nice too," Sister Tomasina said.

"Why would anyone want to spill out or take the paints? Are you sure those cans were not empty before?" Father asked again, looking directly at me.

"Of course I'm sure!" Now I was really getting angry. I was real tempted to say what I saw and what I thought was the truth, and I kept hoping that Danny and Saida might back me up. I looked at them, but they didn't say anything. Ismael was acting real calm and cool. He was the first one to speak out.

"I was right here working all the time and I didn't see anybody."

"I did go to the bathroom," Danny said, "but I came right back."

"I didn't see anyone either. I just went to wash up after I finished my work," said Saida.

"That's it for today, kids," Father Gabriel said. "We'll hope to have the paint for you by the time you come back to work. In the meantime we'll ask around, search some more, and try to get to the bottom of this. Six cans half full of paint do not evaporate by themselves!"

At home that evening I told Tio what happened and he listened quietly as he always did.

"Tio, I know it's them. When I saw Anita and Marta laughing and all secretive, I had this creepy feeling that something was wrong."

"But if they took the paint, they would be hurting their own church and the play, in fact the whole carnival! And that's very stupid. Don't you think so?"

"I know. That shows how much they hate me. I mean I was willing to forget all that happened and be friends, but no, not them. They just have a grudge against me."

"Listen"—Tio Jorge paused—"I don't think they hate you. They just resent you, Felita, because you are an outsider. In that way this place has not changed much. People around here don't like or trust strangers, especially city people. Another thing, you just joined the center and already you are making stage sets and are practically in charge of the scenery. They must resent that too."

"Well, I'd still like to tell Father about what I saw and what I think."

"Never mind, Felita, I think you were right not to say anything, because like Ismael said, you have no proof. If you accused them, it would just be your word against theirs. There are three of them and only one of you, and they have been here longer than you. Besides, they're getting more paint, and you will be able to finish the sets. You'll see, I'm sure they won't bother you again. Forget about it, Felita, just make some great sets and then these girls will turn ugly and green with envy."

That night I couldn't sleep. It had been a while since I had felt this bad. The idea that someone might want to hurt me so badly that they would try to mess up the sets sent a sharp ache right through my insides. Why wouldn't those girls get off my back? I was tired of defending myself here, just like I was tired of defending myself back home when I was in a white neighborhood and they called me names too. It all felt wrong. It wasn't fair. As I lay in my bed suddenly I had this feeling that I was in the middle of nowhere.

I thought of home. If I were there now, I'd be going to Jones Beach, Coney Island, or maybe to the Bronx Zoo. I'd be hanging out a lot. I'd go to street fairs, block parties, and to the free concerts in the park. There were all kinds of great things to do. I know Mami would let me stay overnight at Gigi's more often now that I was older. And when I thought of Vinny, I got this great warm feeling all over my body. I remembered the last time he kissed me when we were sitting in that little park after school and my heart started pounding away. I prayed he'd answer my letter real soon. All of a sudden I missed everybody so much—the kids on my block, even little Joanie. I wanted to go home, where I belonged. I didn't fit in here.

My abuelita had always said how wonderful Puerto Rico was and how I should be proud of being Puerto Rican. Tonight for the first time I had the feeling it was nothing but a pack of lies. Why didn't she tell me how I was gonna be made to feel like an outsider in her own village? If it weren't for Provi, I'd really be miserable.

"Abuelita, this is not the Puerto Rico you promised me! What have you got to say to me now?"

When me and Provi discussed what happened, she agreed that Anita and her gang had taken the paint. "I'm sure it was them," said Provi. "They're in back of this whole business."

"Right, but we can't prove it!"

"That Gladys," she said. "What a fink! I can't believe we used to be so tight. But I think Ismael might be mixed up in this too."

"You do?"

"Yes. When Gladys and me were friends and"—Provi blushed and looked away—"she got her period, her mother became real strict with her. She had to know where Gladys was every minute. Now here's the thing—Ismael was Gladys's boyfriend, and when they wanted to be together, she kept asking me to lie for her. You know, to say she was with me when she was really meeting him. I said no, no way was I gonna be caught and punished for lying. Gladys called me a baby and said I wasn't her good friend anymore."

"Wow! Is Gladys still going with him?"

"No, not anymore. Listen to what happened. Anita took Ismael away from Gladys and he became her boyfriend. When that happened, Gladys came back trying to be my friend again. We made up, but we never became good friends like before. Then Gladys starts hanging around with Anita to be near Ismael because she still likes him and everybody knows it."

"Is Ismael still Anita's boyfriend?"

"I'm sure of it. But you see, Felita, around here the girls are real secretive about having boyfriends because if your parents find out, you never, ever get to see the boy you like. Plus you are watched every minute! It's almost like being in jail."

"What a mess! But, you know something, that's a lot like what happens to us girls back home." I told Provi about how my mother used to guard me and about all Mami's speeches.

"Well, nothing that you've said so far, Felita, makes it sound as strict as it is here. In fact your mother seems to me like she's way more lenient than the mothers here."

"I guess that's true." All of a sudden I felt lucky compared to Provi. For the first time I realized that maybe Mami wasn't so bad after all.

"You know what I'm thinking, Felita? If Ismael is still Anita's boyfriend, which I'm sure is the case, that's why he defended them and is on their side."

"Well, like Tío Jorge said, we are getting more paint and I'm gonna finish my sets, so they went through all that trouble for nothing."

When we all got back to work the next day, we saw there were five quarts of paint, the same colors as before, as well as a gallon of white.

"We couldn't get as much paint," Brother Osvaldo said, "so stretch it as best as you can. And there's something else—one of you four kids is to be here at all times. If one of you has to leave and no one is around, come inside and we'll get someone out here right away. We have to guard this place. I'm sorry to say we haven't found out much. But until we do, we are going to be very careful and watchful. Understand?"

By this time there was only one week left before the carnival. We had a lot to do and everyone was getting excited. I was assigned a part in the play as a Taino woman. I didn't have any of my own lines. At the end I was supposed to recite some lines with the whole group on stage. I wasn't really nervous because I figured there was a bunch of us speaking together and so if I forgot my lines, it wouldn't matter much.

Tio Jorge called our relatives in San Juan and invited them to come to the play. Now that I knew my whole family in Puerto Rico would be there, I was fussier than ever about the sets.

Danny and Saida were good about doing what I told them to do, but Ismael was still giving me a hard time. We had it out when I asked him to paint a dark green outline on the palm leaves, so they would look more real. Ismael refused.

"I got more important work to do for Danny." I went over to check with Danny, who said that Ismael could work with me.

I asked Ismael again. "Get lost!" he said. That's all I had to hear! It was bad enough Ismael had probably helped Anita and them take our paint, but there was no way he was going to get away with not doing his work!

I stood right in front of him with a brush and a bucket. "Now, you stop it, Ismael, and help me right now!" I was shouting so loud, I figured the whole courtyard could hear me. Ismael jumped back. "What's more important to you anyway? Giving me a hard time, or getting this scenery done right? I'm in charge here, Danny and Saida know it, and you damn well know it too!"

Ismael just stared at me like he couldn't believe what I was doing or saying. "Now, I can't do this job all by myself, so here!" I handed him the brush and bucket. "Take it!" For a moment he didn't move, but then he reached over, took what I gave him, and went right to work. Now that everybody was working at full speed, I was sure our sets were gonna turn out perfect.

Two days before the big event, we worked on the last details of the set. It all looked very wonderful. There was now a whole Taino village on stage, with farm animals, and yucca and corn growing in the fields. In the background Tainos were playing an ancient ballgame and behind them was the shoreline and the sea beyond it. We had used every last drop of paint.

"It looks so real—the Taino people and the village," Mrs. Quintero, the woman in charge of the costumes, called out. She even got up on stage to examine the paintings. "Wonderful!"

"Great job you all did!" Judy and Irene waved to us as they walked by with a bunch of other kids.

That evening everyone was in a wonderful mood. Father Gabriel spoke to all the kids at the center. "We should be pleased and very proud of what we have accomplished. I want to compliment and congratulate all the people who worked on the scenery. Felita, who just came to us this summer, has worked very hard and done a great job and so have all the others who helped." Danny, Saida, Ismael, and me looked at each other, feeling like close buddies, knowing how we had all finally cooperated.

I looked around at the smiling faces and suddenly saw Anita, Marta, and Gladys. They looked real quiet and angry. Tough, I thought. I couldn't help feeling good seeing them all so miserable, because in spite of what they'd done, we got through on time.

When I got home, I found two letters waiting for me from Vinny and Gigi. I called Provi and she persuaded her father to drive her over so I could share them with her.

First I read her Vinny's letter. It was real long and said that he'd done a lot of sightseeing with his family, and that he hung out on our block. But the best part, which we read three times, was when he said he missed me and couldn't wait to see me and that most definitely he was still my boyfriend.

Then I read her Gigi's letter, which said she'd gone to the movies a lot, to Central Park, and to the beach. She also said I should say hello to my new friend Provi and ask her to come to New York City to visit.

Suddenly Provi looked real sad. "I'm going to miss you so much," she said.

"Me too. Listen, why *don't* you come to New York and stay with me? My room isn't as big as yours, but we can still fit in. I can show you around, and you can meet all my friends."

"Wow. New York City!" Provi's eyes opened wide. "After all you told us, I'm dying to see it and meet your friends. Tell me again what Vinny looks like and the part about how you met and about the first time he kissed you. Please, I love that story." I repeated all the parts she wanted to hear. "I feel like I know him, Gigi, and all the kids on your block," said Provi when I was done.

"Right," I said, "so will you come visit me?"

"Let's see. Will you take me to the Museum of Natural History?"

"Yes!"

"Central Park?"

"Sure."

"Will you show me some snow?"

"Absolutely!"

"Then I swear I will, cross my heart!"

All this made me feel closer to Provi than ever before.

The next day Provi's father drove us down to Santa Teresa's for the final dress rehearsal. When we arrived, I saw a large crowd gathering around the stage and heard loud voices. I sensed something was wrong.

"Let me by." I began pushing past the crowd. "Let me pass." When I got through, what I saw sent a chill down to the pit of my stomach. Someone had taken black paint and printed the words GRINGITA GO HOME across the ball-playing scene that I had worked on so hard and long. I couldn't speak for a long while;

I was frozen still. Tears began to pour down my face.

Brother Osvaldo came over. "Felita, this is a terrible thing that's happened. I don't know who could have done this and why."

"It was because of me!" All of a sudden I was screaming. "They spoiled everything because they hate me! How could they do this?" I began to cry. By now I was out of control and so angry that I ran over to Ismael, who was standing with Danny and Saida. "Where are they? You know they did it. You know it!"

"What is Felita saying?" asked Sister Pilar. "Who did it?"

"He knows!" I began looking around for Anita, Marta, and Gladys. I was screaming and crying, running around pushing people out of the way. I could hear everybody asking questions and talking at once. I ran back to Ismael, who looked very scared. "They aren't here, are they? Where are they? Where?" I screamed.

Brother Osvaldo grabbed me.

"Felita, stop, stop it! Now, who are you talking about?" Brother asked. "Tell me right now!"

"Anita! That's who! Anita, Marta, and Gladys. And him!" I pointed to Ismael. I really wanted to smack him. "You too, Ismael. You were supposed to be my friend working on our sets. I know you were in with them—you—" I couldn't talk anymore because I was too angry and I kept on crying too much.

Ismael just stood and stared at me. Sister Tomasina came over and held me.

"Ismael, is this true?" Brother Osvaldo asked. "What is Felita saying, eh? That you, Anita, Marta, and Gladys did this?"

"Yes." I swallowed and took a deep breath. "They took the paint. I saw them standing in the back of the building that night. I wanted to say something, but he wouldn't let me. Go on, Ismael, just say it's not true, I dare you!"

"Calm yourself, daughter, calm yourself." Father Gabriel came over and stood with Sister Tomasina and me. "I think we all better go inside, come on. The rest of you, wait here till we're done." Danny, Saida, Ismael, and me followed the grown-ups into Father's office.

Father sat at his desk, then told us all to sit down too. "Now what is going on here?" He looked at Danny. "I want you to tell me what you know."

"Father, that night the paint was missing, Felita said she saw something funny." Danny went on to tell them what I suspected. "But then nobody had proof and—"

Even though I couldn't stop crying and Sister Tomasina kept on rubbing my back, I had to say something. "Sure, but if you all remember, the only person alone by the sets that night was Ismael." Everyone looked at Ismael, who was quiet and staring wide-eyed.

"All right, now what's going here, Ismael?" Brother Osvaldo asked in an angry voice. We all waited. Ismael looked very scared.

"I—I didn't mean to go this far. I didn't think they would do it—" Ismael began to cry.

"All right, Ismael, come on inside to my office," Brother Osvaldo said. "I want to talk to you alone."

When they were gone, Father looked at me. "Now you, Felita, calm yourself. You hear? I want you to tell us all that you know about this. But first no more crying and no more hysterics. Take a deep breath and when you are ready, start."

I did what Father said. Sister Tomasina gave me a tissue. Then I blew my nose, calmed down, and told them everything that had happened.

"Well, since Anita, Marta, and Gladys are not here today, I'm calling up their parents right now," said Father. "Everybody sit and relax. Just take it easy till I finish." He made the phone calls and all the parents said their children were sick with an upset stomach. Father Gabriel told the parents something very serious had happened and that their children were involved. He said he expected to talk to them as soon as possible.

After a while Brother Osvaldo came back with Ismael, whose eyes were real red and swollen from crying. Brother looked so mad, I thought he was gonna slap Ismael. "He told me the whole thing. I can't believe it, but those kids took the paint from the cans. And then last night they came and wrote those disgraceful words on the panel. And do you know why? All because Anita was having a feud with Felita and they were angry at her. I can't believe it!" Brother turned around and whacked Ismael across the back of his head. Ismael closed his eyes and put his hands over his head. "I'm taking him to his parents right now and then I'm paying the others a visit." He took Ismael by the elbow. "You march right into my office and stay there. Don't move until I come to get you, understand? Now go!" Ismael left quickly and quietly.

"I just spoke to the parents," Brother Osvaldo told Father Gabriel, "and all three girls are home with upset stomachs. All too convenient."

"All right," Sister Pilar said. "I think it's time to figure out what to do about the damaged sets and let everyone know what's happened."

In the recreation room people sat on couches, tables and even on the floor; the room was filled. By now I had stopped crying. But Sister Tomasina still sat with me and every once in a while she'd rub my back. Father Gabriel told everyone who had been responsible, and then Brother Osvaldo spoke.

"The damage that was done is not going to affect the carnival in any serious way. What we could do is just remove the damaged panel, but that would make the sets look uneven. Now, as the director of scenery, I know that the set can be repaired. But it's

going to take hard work. What do you say, Felita?"
I didn't know what to answer because I hadn't even
thought about fixing the panel.

"Maybe, I don't know." I was hoarse from so
much crying.

"Good." Brother put his arm around my shoulders.
"Felita, everyone knows that you have done most of
the drawing and painting and we can't repair the
damage without your help. But Danny and Saida will
pitch in all they can, right?" They said yes. "And
I'll do what I can to help too. We'll get more materials—whatever is needed. All of us right here will
scrape up the money."

"That's right," people said. "We sure will." It
seemed that everyone was in favor of Brother's idea.

"What do you say, Felita, will you help too?" I
looked around at Father, Brother, the sisters, and at
all the people that I had worked with and gotten to
know these past few weeks. And I saw that they
all looked as upset as me. For the first time since I'd
come to Santa Teresa's, I felt like I belonged and
that I was with friends instead of strangers.

"I'll do the very best I can," I promised.

After we collected some money and got all the
necessary materials, Danny, Saida, Brother Osvaldo,
and me worked as hard as we could patching up the
damaged panel. I was never more grateful for quick-
drying paint. We all worked late into the night until
we felt we had done all we could. In the end the panel

looked okay, even though it would never be as good as the original.

"It looks beautiful!" Sister Tomasina breathed a sigh of relief along with the rest of us.

By the time I got home I was too tired to think. I told Tio what happened, but wasn't able to answer too many of his questions very clearly. All I wanted was to get some sleep.

The next day I overslept and Tio Manuel had to drive fast to get me to church on time. When I arrived, the final run-through of the play was starting. I rushed to put on my Taino costume and joined the others on stage. It was all getting pretty hectic. As soon as we finished rehearsing, we heard the first cars driving in. Every time I looked at the patched-up scenery, my heart sank a little. It was noticeable because all the other panels were so much smoother and brighter. But I couldn't worry about that now.

"Everybody ready!" said Sister Tomasina. "We will go straight to the back of the stage. No looking around for friends or relatives. No calling out or waving to anybody. Get ready—go!"

We stood in the shade at the back of the stage. I was so nervous I could feel the sweat soaking into my costume. We could hear people talking, babies crying, a couple of dogs barking, and the musicians tuning up. Finally we heard them play the first number. After the applause, Father made his speech. He told them our purpose for the carnival and the theme.

"We have a proud ancestry on this Island. We are descendants not only of the Spaniards, or the Africans who were brought here by force, but of indigenous Island people as well. Today we present a historical dramatization titled *Taino Culture from 1490 Through 1517.*"

That was our cue. I went on stage with the other actors and actresses, taking my place in the back. I was supposed to be grinding flour to make bread. Then the main characters came out and the play was on. When I was feeling less nervous, I looked at the audience and almost fainted. There was Abuelo Juan, Abuela Angelina, Aunt Iraida, Uncle Tomás, and Lina, all smiling and waving at me. I turned away and went on with making make-believe bread, listening carefully for my cues so I'd know when to move. We were now at the end of the first act, after the Spaniards leave, planning to come back to kill the Tainos and take their gold. I waited for Julian, who played Aguebaya, a great chief, to say the last lines.

"These white men may be sacred spirits sent to us by the great god of the sea Huracan. When they return, we will have presents of gold to please them." There was a drumroll and we quickly left the stage.

Sister Tomasina led us back again to the main building. "This is intermission, we have fifteen minutes, so rest and enjoy your break. You were all wonderful, now let's do even better in the last act."

I looked out the window to find out who else in

my family had come. I saw Tio Jorge seated with Tia Maria and Tio Manuel. Sister Tomasina took us to the back of the stage where we waited for the musicians to finish their song. Then on cue we went on the stage. As I played my part I knew the audience was enjoying the play because everyone was paying close attention. In the next scene the Tainos hold a Spanish soldier underwater to see if he lived or drowned. When he died, they knew that the Spaniards were not gods but mortals like them. Chief Aguebaya shouted, "Now we will fight for our liberty or perish in the battle." The Tainos preferred suicide to a life of slavery. In the play I was one of the people who drank poison and then fell dead on the stage. After this there was a battle. The Spaniards finally won and all the Tainos who didn't kill themselves were captured. When that happened the rest of us rose from the dead and chanted together,

"Tainos won the right to the honor roll of history: The way they fell was not the way of cowards."

The musicians played a loud drumroll and the play was over.

The audience kept on applauding and some people shouted, "Bravo!"

"Wonderful! Beautiful!" We all took lots of bows, and then quickly left the stage and hurried back inside to put on our regular clothes. We were delirious with joy because everything had gone so good. After us girls got our clothes on, we all started hugging and kissing. Then the boys came over and we began to hug with them and shake hands. Everybody was congratulating everybody else. When Danny came over, he held me real tight for a long time and gave me a quick kiss on the mouth. "I like you a whole lot, Felita."

I looked at Danny, surprised. I guess we had all been working so hard, I never noticed he liked me. I looked at him now feeling so self-conscious that I knew I must be blushing. Danny is not as handsome as Vinny; he's shorter and wears glasses. But he has lots of curly brown hair and a great smile. "See you later, Felita, maybe we can get together later during the carnival today," he said.

"Sure." Wait till I tell Provi! I thought.

Outside I found my folks waiting for me. Uncle Tomás had a camera and began taking pictures of all of us. Lina was jumping up and down like she was on a trampoline or something. "Felita, I love you. You were so good."

"Felita," said Aunt Julia, "Uncle Mario and the boys couldn't make it. They had tickets for a big ball game and they took Carlito with them. But I'm here; it was just fabulous! Wait till I write your mother and tell her. She will be so proud of you."

"What does my granddaughter want?" Abuelo Juan asked. "Just say the word. I'm so proud. Wasn't she something? And she painted all of that by her-self."

"Abuelo, I did have some help, you know," I said. He was getting me so embarrassed, I was glad none of my friends were around.

"They seem to like you so much here, Felita," said Aunt Julia. I wasn't going to mention the paint, or anything else that had happened. I was just happy our play was a big success and that we were all here together. I went off to find Provi and took Lina with me. Provi was with her parents, Diana, Raymond, Gino, and a whole bunch of other relatives. They introduced me around, but there were so many of them, I couldn't remember who was who. In fact the whole courtyard was so crowded with people that you could hardly move. They were eating and really enjoying themselves. The band played fast music and couples were dancing. Provi, Lina, Gino, and me took off to spend the money we had gotten from the grown-ups.

"Guess what?" I said, and then I told Provi about what had happened earlier with Danny.

"Wow. Did he really kiss you, Felita?"

"Right on the mouth."

"Do you like him?"

"He is cute, but Vinny's my boyfriend. Vinny, remember?"

"Sure, but he's not here," Provi said. "Let's see if

we can find Danny and the others." We searched around until we found Saida, Judy, Danny, and Julian. Then we hung out with them and bought all kinds of snacks and played games. Danny mostly stayed close to me. When he won the game where you knock over the wooden bottles, he gave me his prize. It was a small furry monkey.

"Here's something for you to remember me by, Felita," he said.

Suddenly we heard Sister Pilar's voice over the loudspeaker, announcing that the carnival was over and it was time to clean up.

Before Danny went off, he spoke to me. "Will you write to me from New York?"

"All right."

"Promise me you won't forget, Felita."

When I promised, he reached over and put a piece of paper with his address in my hand, holding on for a long time.

"This here is for sure a huge mess," Provi complained as we worked putting tons of garbage into big plastic bags. After a while things started looking orderly and clean again. Provi and me were just about the last ones left. Everyone had already said their good-byes. Now we were waiting for Provi's father to take us home. I looked up at the repaired panel and thought of all that had happened. "Provi, what do you think they'll do to Anita and the others?" I asked.

"Oh, listen, my mother is good friends with Gladys's mother, and I heard that they are all going to be punished by their parents. But the worst part is that they won't be able to be members of the youth center anymore. You see, Felita, there's nothing else to do around this area. I'm sure you know that by now."

"True," I agreed. "But I am kind of sorry for Ismael because he was nice at the end. He worked hard and I know he was proud of what we did. I just know it."

"Yeah? You can be sorry, but remember he was in on it with them all along."

"I guess you're right about him. But I'm glad that Anita, Marta, and Gladys got theirs. For them, I don't feel at all sorry."

"Provi! Felita!" We heard Mr. Romero, Provi's father, calling us. "It's time to go. Come on!"

"Now I suppose all the sets have to come down," I said.

"Maybe they'll save them," said Provi.

"Maybe." I took a last long look at the scenery before I turned and left with Provi.

Now that the play and carnival were over at Santa Teresa's, I had more time for myself, so I went with Tio to see his property.

"You are going to be surprised at all that's been done since you last were here," said Tio. He showed me where the foundation for the house was and where the workmen were busy putting in the well. "I told my niece that we are going to have a little piece of paradise here," he said to them.

"It will be something special, Don Jorge," the foreman said. After Tio showed me every inch of what was being done, we walked over to the side of the mountain, which looked out over a wide view.

"I only wish Amanda, your abuelita, was here. She would have loved this." For a moment I thought Tio was going to cry.

"I'll bet she is here, right now in spirit. Looking at us and smiling," I said. I felt so sorry for Tio and wanted to comfort him; knowing that I was leaving him made it even worse.

"I want you to know that you and your brothers are very important to me. But I feel that you, Felita, even more than Johnny or Tito, are my very own child, and in a special way, my future." I hugged Tio and we held onto each other.

"Tio, I'd like to take a little walk, is that all right?"

"Sure, I've got to check on a few things with the foreman."

As I walked and breathed all the sweet smells of the morning air, I began to look at everything differently. Just knowing I was leaving and wouldn't be able to see these mountains every day and go for my walks with Provi made everything around me seem much more special. I knew I was going to miss my life here. For one thing I had gotten used to my peace and quiet and my privacy, none of which I had back home. Then there were my friends, especially Provi. I hated leaving her. She had been as good to me as Gigi. I also thought of Danny. Even though he wasn't as cute as Vinny, he was smart and liked me a lot. Plus he was a good artist and understood how I felt about art. I knew this by how well we worked together. Suddenly I felt really sad about leaving here.

I found a good place to sit down on the edge of a steep ridge. The sky was bright blue all the way to the horizon. Little butterflies danced about, then settled onto a bunch of tiny purple flowers. Abuelita used to say that butterflies bring good luck. I hadn't thought about my grandmother for a long time and then I remembered how angry I had been at her during my troubles with Anita at the center. Now I wanted Abuelita to know everything was all right. I got up and began looking for wildflowers. I picked as many different kinds as I could find. Soon I had a bouquet of orange, white, purple, bright yellow, red, and pink flowers. Then I added some green and purplish leaves. When I was satisfied, I tied my bouquet with a long strip of palm leaf. I stopped in front of a large flamboyan tree bursting with brilliant red blossoms, and there at the bottom, against its trunk, I set down my bouquet.

"Do you remember Abuelita, that after you went away forever, I promised if I came to Puerto Rico, I'd pick lots of wildflowers for you? Well, here they are. I love you very much, Abuelita."

After Mass at Santa Teresa's on Sunday, I had a chance to talk with some of the kids before I said good-bye. It was definite that Anita, Marta, Gladys, and Ismael had been kicked out. Also their parents had to pay for all the extra paint and supplies that had to be purchased on account of what they did. But no one knew for sure how they were or how they were going to get punished by their parents. Saida promised to write me as soon as she found out anything. Danny said as soon as he heard from Ismael, he'd write to me too. I could see he was feeling bad about my leaving. Father called us all over to the church steps, then Sister Pilar spoke to me. "Felita," she said in her gruff voice, "listen. I think I speak for everyone here, including Father and the young people, when I say we want you to return soon. Don't you forget your Puerto Rican family here on the Island once you return to the big city, you hear? You are one of us now and we want you back not just for the summer but for at least a year or two. After all, it's not always that we have such a talented artist amongst us." With that she gave me a hug and then everyone started to say good-bye, wishing me luck and asking me to come back soon.

I tried not to cry as I walked away and looked over at where our sets had been. All that was left of our stage was the platform. I wanted to go back and ask them what they had done with everything, but instead I waved good-bye and followed Tia Maria and Tio Manuel to the car.

When we got back, Tia Maria started grumbling. "There's lots to do and you only have two days left. I am not sending you to your mother with dirty clothes. I have washing and ironing, plus all your stuff to get packed. It never ends with you." I guess I was getting used to her because I wasn't even angry. Most of what she said went in one ear and out the other. She actually had been pretty nice to me. Like the whole time I was working on the sets, and when all the trouble was happening, she never once got on my case. But more than anything I was beginning to understand that unless Tia Maria had something to complain about—anything—she wouldn't be happy.

The following day Provi and me spent the afternoon together hanging out, going for our walk, and rereading the letters I had gotten from Gigi and Vinny.

"Don't forget," I told her, "you are coming to visit me real soon." We began to talk about New York City again and about all the things we were going to do together. Up until now I had been unhappy about going home, but as we talked I began getting excited.

"I can't wait to visit all those places you talked about and meet Gigi and Vinny," she said.

"You will have a great time, Provi. I can't wait to see them myself. Imagine, in just a few days I'll be home—on my block with my friends."

"I'll miss you, Felita. Please write to me."

"You know I will, Provi. I'll write to you and tell you everything that's going on with me."

"Good, and I'll write back giving you all the news

from here." We both hugged and felt much better.

That night Diana and Raymond cooked a fabulous dinner. We all had a great time, eating, listening to music, and just talking.

"What time are you leaving tomorrow?" asked Diana.

"My uncle is picking me up in the afternoon," I said. "I sure wish I could be here when your baby is born. Please write and tell me whether it's a boy or a girl, and please send pictures."

"Will you remember me when you are in New York City, Felita?" asked Gino. I felt like I was leaving my own family. There was no way I would ever forget them.

"Of course I will," I told them. "I'll remember all of you."

It was my last day in Barrio Antulio. In the afternoon, after Tia Maria had packed all of my things and served us lunch, Tio Jorge and me sat in the back patio of our cottage. We were waiting for Uncle Tomás to pick me up. Tio was quiet. I could see he was feeling sad. I was feeling sad too. I had gotten used to being with Tio Jorge. Before, when I was younger, I mostly talked to my abuelita and never got to know him. But now I realized how much I loved Tio. He had been real good to me this summer. He had backed me up against Tia Maria, and never told me where I had to be or what I had to do, especially after our agreement. In fact I felt freer with Tio Jorge than I did at home with Mami and Papi.

"Tio," I said, breaking the silence, "I hope you won't be too lonely without me."

"Lonely, me? With all the work I have ahead of me? Building a house, getting the animals, and also working on my nature collection again. I'll have plenty to do, never you mind."

"Tio, I had a great time here. I'm gonna miss my new friends, and"—I looked at him—"and I'm gonna miss you very much."

He smiled, then reached out and held my hand. "You belong here, Felita, just like I do. This is your Island and your home. You must never forget that. No matter what anyone tells you. Do you understand?"

"Yes."

"Good," said Tio Jorge. "Now I think I hear Tomás's car. Let's get ready."

As we were putting my suitcases in the car, Tia began crying and making such a fuss over me.

"We are gonna miss you," said Tio Manuel, "it's been good for Maria to have a young one here to worry about and take care of."

"Here you are," said Tia Maria, pressing a set of rosary beads into my hand. "These are very old. They belonged to an aunt of mine. Use them during Mass and they will bring you luck." I was surprised that she'd done this. I knew the beads were her favorite ones because she always took them to Sunday Mass. I thanked her and we kissed good-bye.

"When you return with the family, we can all be together in the new house," said Tio Jorge, hugging me. "Tell them I'll be sending pictures so you can all see how the place is coming along."

I had already said good-bye to the animals out back, but as I was about to get into the car I saw Yayo the rooster standing nearby, staring at me. "Good-bye, Yayo, and behave yourself for a change, you hear?" I waved and threw him a kiss and right away he starts coming toward me. But this time I knew what he was up to, so I just picked up my hand and he took off in the other direction.

Visiting Abuelo Juan and Abuela Angelina in San Juan took away some of the sadness I felt about leaving. There were always a lot of people coming in and out of their house. Lina and Carlito came by, and Aunt Iraida took us to the big shopping malls. Then I went to Aunt Julia's and swam at the beach. Everyone kept asking me how I liked staying in Tio's village. I told them all about Provi, about making the scenery for the play, and about my new friends. But I never mentioned the trouble I had. I didn't want to talk about it because really I wished it had never happened.

"Look, in the future you must stay longer with us

right here," said Abuelo Juan. "I know that you love your Tio Jorge, but after all, I have as much of a right to see my granddaughter as anyone else! Now, tell me what you think of Puerto Rico, Felita."

"Abuelo, I love it so much and I want to come back."

"Wonderful." He was real pleased. "That makes me so happy. I can hear you are now speaking Spanish almost like a true Puerto Rican. You tell your brothers, my grandsons, that they better start learning Spanish too! You hear?"

The day I had to leave, most of my family loaded up into two cars and drove me to the airport. Aunt Julia gave me instructions on how I had to pick up three boxes for Mami when I got to the airport in New York. Everyone kept hugging and kissing me until it was time to get on the plane. Aunt Julia made sure I got a window seat and told the airline clerk that I was traveling alone and to take care of me.

The ride home was smooth and quiet. After lunch I took a nap, and when I woke up, I turned to the lady sitting next to me.

"Do you know the time?" I asked her.

"I'm sorry," she said, "but I don't speak Spanish." I hadn't even noticed that I was talking in Spanish.

"Excuse me," I said in English, "do you know the time?"

"It's three o'clock. We'll be landing in less than half an hour."

"Thanks." I yawned and stretched out.

"You speak English very well. Have you ever been to New York before?" she asked me.

"Yes, I was born there."

"Oh." I could see she was embarrassed.

"In fact," I went on, "I've been visiting Puerto Rico and staying with my uncle up in the mountains."

"Did you have a good time?"

"Yes, I had a wonderful time. I enjoyed myself a lot."

"Are you sorry, then, or happy to be going back to New York City?"

"I guess I'm sorry to be leaving but happy to be going home." As soon as that lady asked me how I felt, I realized I was having such strange feelings. One minute I was sad and then I remembered I was going to see Vinny and Gigi and all my friends and I got happy. I wondered where it was I wanted to be most. In P.R or home in New York City? Then I remembered Vinny's letter tucked away in my suitcase. Vinny and me were going to junior high with a bunch of my other friends. Junior high school, with no little kids running around! I thought of my parents and my brothers, and all the kids on my block. I couldn't wait to tell everyone about the great summer I had—about the beaches, the sightseeing, and the play. And best of all, I could tell my family, Gigi, and Vinny about Anita, Marta, Gladys, and Ismael and how it had finally turned out so good. All of a sudden I couldn't wait to get home!

After the plane landed and I got to the luggage claim section, I saw Papi waiting for me.

"Papi! Papi!" I went running over to him. Papi picked me up and I could feel his strong arms as he lifted me up in the air.

"Felita, mi hijita. How you have grown! You are so tall and so beautiful. Look at you! You are as brown as a coconut! Wait until your mother sees you." We got my suitcases and the boxes Aunt Julia had sent and headed straight for Mami, Johnny, and Tito. Mami came rushing over, threw her arms around me, and gave me a real tight hug and lots of kisses.

"Dios mio, my baby. Look at you!" She kept on staring at me. "I left a little girl in Puerto Rico and now I get back a young lady. Felita, I couldn't get used to being at home without you. I missed you something terrible! Now, tell me, did you have a good time? Honest? How's Tio Jorge? And Tia Maria and Tio Manuel? I know you just spent a few days with your grandfather. How's Abuelo Juan? You have to tell us everything, everything, you hear!"

"Good to have you back," Johnny said, and we kissed and hugged.

"Hey, you are looking less ugly," said Tito as he gave me a hug. "You must've done something good. Keep it up and you might get pretty. Right, Mami?"

Everyone laughed. That was my brother Tito, all right. He was a character, and that was for sure!

"So, how did you find living back in the mountains of Puerto Rico?" Papi asked. "Did you find enough things to do there? It wasn't too boring, was it, Felita?"

"It was great!" I said.